THE TEACUP WITH THE WRONG HANDLE

By Liora Dawn

Copyright

Ink & Ivy Village Mysteries Series Book One.
The Teacup with the Wrong Handle
© 2025 Liora Dawn. All rights reserved.

No part of this book may be reproduced, stored in a retrieval system, or transmitted in any form or by any means, electronic or mechanical, including photocopying and recording, without prior written permission from the publisher, except for brief quotations used in reviews and critical articles.

This is a work of fiction. Names, characters, organisations, places, and incidents either are products of the author's imagination or are used fictitiously. Any resemblance to actual persons, living or dead, or to actual events or locales is coincidental.

First edition

Cover and interior: TBD
Editing: TBD

Published by Liora Dawn Books
Printed in the country of purchase

Dedication

For cozy readers, who prize a fair clue, a warm cup, and a village that minds its manners. You keep the kettle on and the pages turning.

A Note From The Author

If this story made you smile or kept you reading past bedtime, please take a moment to leave a short, honest review on your favourite store or Goodreads. Even a single sentence helps other readers find Tessa, Mabel, Bramble, and the next case. Thank you.

Contents

The Teacup with the Wrong Handle
Copyright
Dedication
A note from the author
One
Two
Three
Four
Five
Six
Seven
Eight
Nine
Ten
Eleven
Twelve
Thirteen
Fourteen
Fifteen
Sixteen
Seventeen
Eighteen
Nineteen
Twenty
Author's Note

ONE

Tessa Harper had timed the ribbon to fall on the stroke of nine. It curled neatly into her palm anyway because Bramble, who did not care for ceremony, nosed it as if checking the knot for structural integrity. He wagged once, satisfied, then trotted to the door where the morning light turned his terrier whiskers into fringe.

Ink & Ivy was open.

The bell above the door chimed; a light, bookish sound she had chosen in a fit of optimism, as though the right ring could summon steady trade and the kind of problems that came with old wood and good stories. Shelves of fountain pens lined the right wall, a fond nod to her years in design, their lacquered barrels catching the light like boiled sweets. The left side held glue caddies, brass polish, cotton gloves, silica gel, and a hand-lettered sign that said Repairs while you wait if I am sure it will hold. She had meant it as a joke, but the village had taken it as a challenge.

"Morning, love," called Mabel Clegg from the threshold, parcel under one arm, opinion under the other. "Brought your first patient."

Tessa smiled. "If it is a patient, I charge extra for bedside manner."

Mabel lifted the parcel onto the counter and peeled back brown paper to reveal a typewriter ribbon tin converted long ago into a button box. Inside, glass buttons glowed like tiny moons. "Lid's loose. I thought you'd have one of your clever glues."

"As luck has it, I stock three." Tessa tipped the lid; the press-fit had gone. "I'll shim it and seal a hairline, nothing more. You will never forgive me if I ruin the patina."

"I've kept it since '68. It was Aunt Ivy's," Mabel said, voice softening. "Seems right you mend it in her shop."

Ink & Ivy had been a name before it was a lease. Tessa's aunt had run a stationery stall at the Fernvale market for years; the shop on Ivy Lane felt like an inevitability, a corner that had been waiting for her all along. She had painted the door a calm green and stencilled ivy along the skirting as a quiet promise to keep old things good.

Bramble huffed. The bell chimed again.

This time it was pace rather than parcel. A young woman in a silk dressing gown under a coat, hair in pins, cheeks high with panic. She flung the door so hard the bell skirled, then clutched a hatbox to her chest as if it held a live bird.

"Are you the glue person?" she asked, a rush of breath in one go. "Please say you are."

"I am a person with glue," Tessa said, calm against the gust she brought in. "And you are about to put that box down before your hands betray you."

The woman obeyed and set the hatbox on the counter. Her fingers trembled; her eyes were the bright of someone who had slept too little and planned too much. She took in the shelves as if a solution might leap out and throw itself at her. "I'm Isla," she said. "My wedding is in two hours and the teacup is wrong."

Mabel leaned, delighted. "At last. Proper drama. Go on."

Isla eased the lid off the hatbox. Inside, on tissue, lay a vintage teacup, bone china fine enough to pass the light. Roses wound along the bowl in tidy swags. It would have been charming if not for the handle, which had been glued on the opposite side from where any sane handle ought to be. The curve sat at a left-leaning angle, slightly proud, as if it dreamed of being correct but had taken a wrong turn.

Tessa bent close. Heat gun; medium bond; decent clamp pressure. The work was neat in one sense and thoughtless in another. Along the join, the glue seam was bright and clean. The porcelain around it showed its age with thin tea ghosts and hairline crazing; the joint did not. She lifted the cup and tilted it to the light. No staining in the joint. Fresh.

She set it down again and, because her nose had been trained by years of pens and solvents, she took in the air above the cup. A faint citrus note hovered; sharper than orange oil, more peel than sweet.

"What did you do to it?" Isla asked, horrified, as if sniffing might knock it out of alignment.

"Breathed," Tessa said. "When did this happen?"

"This morning. It fell. I mean it toppled off the dresser during photos. The handle snapped clean. My planner, Delia, said it was fine, she knew someone who could fix anything in five minutes, and then someone did, and now it is wrong, and all the photo setups for the tea table will look odd because the saucers are set, and I cannot hold it with my hand the way we planned." The words piled up, tripped, and kept going. "The saucer matches, but it is at the hall. My sister Poppy is sitting on it like a dragon because she thinks I will smash it."

"Prudent of her," Mabel said, approving. "Sisters are useful for sitting on things."

Isla pulled in air. "Can you put it back where it belongs?"

Tessa measured the angle with her eye. The handle had been reattached for a left-dominant hold. She could, in principle, remove the fresh joint and reset. But to do it properly she would need time, solvent, a gentle soak, and the sense to keep the heat even so the glaze did not lift. She had an hour and fifty minutes and a bride breathing like a steam kettle.

"I can try," she said, careful. "But I will not promise. Whoever glued this used a fast set. The joint is clean, which helps, and it is new, which helps more. I will need to persuade it off without tearing the porcelain. If I fight it, we risk a shard."

Isla's eyes flashed. "Do not fight it. Charm it."

"Always my preference," Tessa said.

She scanned the bench. Citrus lingered above the cup; her own solvents were capped and labelled; she had not opened anything yet. That scent had walked in with the hatbox. She fixed the idea to a pin in her mind, then reached for cotton swabs and a small bottle of neutral softener rather than her citrus-based cleaner. The irony was not lost on her.

A shadow fell across the glass. A boy on a bicycle had braked hard at the window; he peered in, then cupped his hands to the glass to shout through. "Miss, you coming? Siren at the hall."

Isla went white. "The hall."

"What sort of siren?" Mabel called back.

"Ambulance," the boy said. "Everyone's running."

Isla looked at the cup as if it might offer advice. "Delia will kill me if I'm late. Or she will kill me twice if I arrive with the wrong handle in all the photos."

"Delia can manage five minutes without you," Mabel said. "Go on, take my arm. I know your mother; she will need a person who can say the right thing."

"Take Bramble," Tessa said to Isla, because a small solid dog can brace a shaking human better than most things. "He is excellent at walking in a straight line."

Isla stared as if presented with a method of walking she had not considered, then nodded and took the lead. "Good dog." She looked back at Tessa, apology and panic in a tangle. "Do what you can. Please."

"I will work and bring it to you," Tessa said. "The Thimble & Fern first or the hall?"

"The hall," Isla said. "We're dressing there. The tea service is laid in the anteroom by the landing. Poppy will be looking for an excuse to shout."

"Then I shall avoid giving her one," Tessa said, which experience had taught was not always possible.

They went out into a village that had tipped from slow morning to alarm in a breath. Fernvale Hall stood at the top of the lane, honey limestone glowing under a sky that had taken the trouble to be a perfect blue. Ribbons showed through the open door. Someone had arranged small lavender posies along the rails. The ambulance lights bounced off old stone and gave the day a stagey feel, wrong in its own way, like the handle.

By the time Tessa reached the steps, Isla had disappeared inside with Bramble trotting, ears pricked. A knot of guests clustered in the entrance, all phones and uncertainty. The faint smell of polish lifted off the landing like a sheen; Len Porter, the caretaker, stood pale by the door with a mop in his hands as if the correct thing to do at all times was mop.

"What happened?" Mabel asked him in a gentler tone than he deserved.

Len swallowed. "I found her. I did the stairs half an hour ago; I swear I put the sign. Delia said it wanted to shine for the photos. She said she'd do the ribbons and the banners herself. I went to the back for the spare bulbs and then I heard someone call, and there she was at the bottom. I didn't even see her fall. I wouldn't have let it happen."

"Where is she?" Tessa asked, quiet.

"In the hall," he whispered. "They moved her near the window for space. Paramedics are with her."

Tessa did not go further than the landing. She had no wish to be in the way and no stomach for invasion. She stood where Len had stood and looked at what Len had not seen. The polish shone like lacquer. The grain of the old boards showed through as waves under ice. On the top landing, before the stair's first edge, a faint skid had marked the gloss; not a scuff from a toe on a step, but a drag and slide where a shoe had lost purchase on level ground. She crouched and looked along the line. The mark began a hand's breadth before the drop, angled toward the rail.

She looked at the rail. On the cap of the newel post, at the height of an anxious hand, a dull patch showed where varnish had thinned. She touched it with one knuckle. Tacky. Not wet, not sticky as syrup; a slight pull, like a countertop swabbed with the wrong cleaner. She lifted her hand to her face. A breath of citrus rose; sharper than orange oil.

Mabel watched her face rather than the floor. "Thoughts."

"Polish," Tessa said. "And a cleaner that does not belong."

"I am always amazed," Mabel said, "at how often people expect floors to behave like scenery."

A paramedic called from inside; a man's voice she did not know. People moved through the doorway to make room. Isla, near the coat stand, had her hands over her mouth. Poppy stood beside her with a look that said she was ready to blame gravity. Tessa did not see Delia's sleek bob, only the outline of a body on the far side of a screen.

Someone touched Tessa's shoulder. It was Len, eyes rimmed red. "I told her to mind the landing," he said, hoarse. "I polished. For the pictures."

Tessa did not say what she thought about the judgement of anyone who polished a landing on a wedding morning. He would be saying it to himself with force before the hour. "Where is your sign?"

"There," he said, and pointed to a caution board folded by the wall, neat as a good intention.

"Did Delia ask you to move it?" Mabel asked.

"She said it was ugly," he whispered. "Said people should look at the flowers, not the sign."

From the hall came the practical music of work; paramedics taking readings, a radio crackling, a second crew stepping through. Tessa stood clear and let her attention rest on small things that spoke without names. The run of the rail was smooth; the banister spindles had been wiped. No dust crescents where fingers had gone. The cap carried a brightness where something had lifted varnish. She breathed in again and felt the sharp citrus at the edge of the polish's softer wax scent.

She looked down the stairwell. The first run dropped to a half landing where a tall window cast squares of light across the steps. A banner had been tied along the rail; pale silk with ivy leaves that echoed the shop she had left ten minutes before. On the landing tiles, where dust should have lived in the grout, the joints were clean. A clump of ribbon lay crushed near the bottom, a pale line pressed into it where a heel had skated.

"Isla," Mabel called gently. "Come here, love."

Isla moved as if underwater. She let Mabel guide her toward a bench near the door. Bramble wedged himself under Isla's knees with the gravity of a small ship. Poppy hovered, both hands fisted.

"What happened?" Poppy demanded of no one. "She was going for the banners. The florist said the ivy lengths needed trimming. Len, why would you polish today of all days?"

"Not now," Mabel said in a tone that had soothed worse.

11

Tessa crouched by Isla. "I will bring the cup when I can. If anyone asks about the saucer, tell them it is safe."

"It is at the hall," Isla said with a ghost of her earlier babble. "The tea is in the anteroom. Delia said everything in sight must match."

Poppy shot a look at the hatbox under Tessa's arm. "If that cup is in the photos the wrong way round, I will die."

"You will not," Isla said, mechanical. "You will live and glare at me for a week."

"Two," Poppy said, then pressed her lips together and wiped her cheek with the heel of her hand.

A police car pulled in behind the ambulance and a tall man stepped out, dark coat, sleeves rolled. His face was composed rather than hard; it had the look of someone who let evidence do the talking. He spoke to the paramedics and to Len, who bobbed and nodded and led him to the landing. He took in the room, the steps, the rail, the caution sign that had not been set, the polish's shine. His gaze went to the newel cap, paused for a beat, then moved on. When his eyes found Tessa's, it was a brief acknowledgement rather than a question. He had the kind of attention that lands where it means to.

He moved away. Tessa stood and gave Isla a handkerchief. "You do not want a tissue in the first photos. This is linen. It will not leave lint."

Isla laughed, a sound that was almost a sob. "Who are you again?"

"Someone who fixes handles," Tessa said. "And looks."

"Are you a detective?" Poppy asked, suspicion on reflex.

"I fix handles," Tessa said again, and made it gentle.

"Delia would have hated this," Isla whispered. "She hated anything untidy."

Tessa had met Delia twice. The woman had a talent for choreography. If flowers could have stood straighter on command, they would have. It was hard to marry the neatness she favoured with a fall on a bright day, but life had never asked permission before it tipped a table.

The paramedics moved; the radio spoke in its clipped tongue. The man in the coat came back to the door and spoke quietly to Isla and Poppy. He introduced himself as Detective Inspector Malik Shaw; his voice was low enough not to carry. He said the right words for the moment. He did not ask questions yet. There would be time for that.

"Do you need me?" Len asked him, raw.

"We will, Mr Porter," Shaw said. "For now, sit."

Len sat on the bottom stair like a boy who had stayed late to put chairs away and found disaster instead of gold stars.

Tessa stepped back to the landing, took one more look at the skid on the gloss, and fixed it in her head the way she pinned colour matches. The mark began before the step. A person had slid, not tripped. There was intent somewhere in the room; either in the choice to polish or in the way someone had used what the polish did. She thought of the citrus she had smelled at the cup, then at the newel cap. Two breaths in two places.

"Time," Mabel murmured.

"Time," Tessa echoed.

She carried the hatbox back to the shop as swiftly as her sense of respect would allow. People watched her pass with the curiosity reserved for anyone who looks as if they know what to do. She did not. She knew how to work, which helped.

Inside Ink & Ivy, the calm returned like a curtain falling. The bell chimed and was quiet. Tessa set the hatbox on the bench, lifted the cup, and angled it so the light from the front window ran along the join. The seam was glossy, clear, a touch heavier where the curve met the bowl. No tea stain had reached into the glue line. Whoever had set it had not faked age. Fast, clean, in a hurry.

She opened the softener and dampened a swab. No citrus. She would not echo the scent she had found on the cup. She tested the edge of the joint with the barest trace of solvent and felt, under the pad, a slight give. Good. She breathed, took her time, and worked a hair's breadth along the join; backward and forward, coaxing rather than prying.

Bramble drank from his bowl, then came to sit at her foot; anchor, metronome, critic. Mabel settled on the stool with the button tin and pretended not to watch.

"Who brings a teacup to a wedding," Mabel said after a moment, "and glues the handle on the wrong side."

"Someone who knows glue but not hands," Tessa said. "Or someone who did not care which hand held it."

"You smelled it, didn't you," Mabel said. "That sharp peel thing."

"I did."

"Same as the rail."

"Yes."

Mabel folded her hands around the button tin. "I do not like coincidences."

"Nor do I," Tessa said, and eased another millimetre of give.

From the street, the murmur rose and fell; the village making sense the way villages do, by walking and saying each other's names. Tessa kept at the joint. Little by little, the handle loosened. When it released, it did so with a sigh rather than a crack. She wrapped the base in cloth, set the handle in a cradle, and turned her attention to the old surface. The glaze where the handle had sat showed a ghost line, helpful now as a guide. She would clean it, then set the handle in its proper place without insisting on perfection. A perfect repair would scream in photographs; a gentle one would sit as if nothing had happened.

She worked the old glue away with care, then scored the new edge with a spar of fine paper, no more than a breath. She rinsed the dust, dried it with warm air, and set clamps within reach. Her hand hovered over three bottles. She chose the one that promised strength with a longer cure; she would not risk a fast set and a fresh mistake. The wedding would have to work around physics.

She seated the handle against its former bed. It fit like a remembered hand. She dabbed adhesive, held the curve in place with her fingers, then eased the clamps snug, not tight. Glue bloomed at the seam as a fine line. She wicked it away with a cotton tip, then checked the angle. This time the handle leaned as it ought, not proud; a right-hand set. She exhaled.

"How long," Mabel asked, as if time might bend for a bride.

"An hour before I dare move it; more before I love it," Tessa said. "We will give it the hour. We will carry it like a feather and hope."

"Isla will prefer hope to any sermon."

Tessa cleaned her bench and put away the solvent she had not used. The citrus stayed in her head, not on her cloth. She wrote a small note for herself on the pad by the till: citrus scent on cup; citrus at rail; polish fresh; skid before step. She added one more line: saucer at hall; Poppy dragon. If a detail lived only in her memory, it sometimes shifted to suit the story a person needed. On paper, it held still.

At ten past ten, the bell rang again and a man in a slate suit stepped in, phone to his ear. He looked like a person who booked rooms by the quarter hour and thought of money as a timetable. He smiled at Tessa with the kind of charm that did not reach his eyes, then said into the phone, "Yes, of course. The Trust will expect something tasteful," and went out again before she had the satisfaction of ignoring him. The door swung shut on the tail of his call. The bell chimed and settled. Mabel made a noise low in her throat.

"That was Martin Hale," she said, dry. "He sits on everything except his hands."

"The Laurel Trust?" Tessa asked.

"Among his ornaments," Mabel said. "Do not look at me. I do not own the gossip; it rents a back room."

Tessa checked the clamps. The joint held its position; the line looked clean. She dabbed one last time, then set the cup on its cushion in the hatbox, padded it with cloth, and closed the lid.

"Ready," she said.

Mabel stood, tucked the button tin back under her arm, and patted Bramble. "We will go with you. One of us will carry the gravity and the other will scowl at anyone who tries to touch."

"Bramble can scowl," Tessa said. "I will carry the gravity."

They stepped out into a village that had shifted from alarm to that quick hush that follows bad news. The ambulance had gone. The police car remained. The hall door stood open, a ribbon snagged on the latch.

Inside, the anteroom felt smaller with grief in it. The tea table, laid with care, waited as if duty could mask absence. Isla sat with her mother. Poppy stood in the doorway with her arms crossed as if barricades could hold back fact. Len had wiped his face and set the caution sign where it should have been in the first place; it looked like a contrition more than a warning now.

Tessa nodded to them, lifted the hatbox lid, and showed Isla the cup. The handle, in its rightful place, made sense to the eye in a way the other had not. Isla pressed her hand to her mouth and then to Tessa's arm.

"You magician," she breathed.

"Fixer," Tessa said. "We will let it cure in peace. No tea near it. It will hold if no one tests it."

"No one will," Poppy said, a promise she sounded able to enforce.

Detective Inspector Shaw stood at the doorway to the landing and watched without interrupting. He had a notepad out but did not write. He was taking in the configuration of people and objects, the way any person with a trained mind does. His gaze moved to the newel cap again, then to the table. Tessa felt the prickle that comes when two thoughts point to the same place. She did not speak the citrus into the room. It was a word for later, not for a family who needed tea and chairs.

Isla's mother lifted her chin. "We will move the ceremony to the garden," she said, voice steady from years of telling small children to stop running. "Delia would have liked that. She hated fuss in a doorway."

There was a rustle of agreement. People who had come to witness vows turned, without rehearsal, into people who move urns and tie ribbons and make room for a different kind of promise. Tessa set the hatbox on a high shelf out of harm's way and left them to their tasks. She stood on the landing one last time and let the room press its facts into her.

Skid before the stair. Fresh polish. Citrus at the rail. Citrus at the cup. A caution sign placed after the worst thing rather than before. And somewhere in the noise, the shape of a decision.

Outside, Bramble pulled her toward the green, then toward Ink & Ivy, then back toward the hall, as if each direction had the same claim. He sneezed, offended by ribbon, then shook it off and trotted on.

"Your nose is better than mine," Tessa told him. "But I had a head start."

The bell chimed when they went back into the shop. The room held the smell of cotton and resin and paper; steady neighbors when the street did not feel steady at all. Tessa wrote one more note and slipped it under the glass on the counter.

Handle reset, right-hand lean. Seam clean. No stain in joint. Faint citrus on arrival.

She closed the pen, set the glue bottle aside, and looked at the stencilled ivy on her skirting. People had a way of making tidy plans and then colliding with the world. She had opened a shop to fix small collisions. Today, the world had offered a larger one. She put the kettle on, because tea saved as many mornings as glue.

The bell chimed yet again.

A woman with a clipboard stepped in, tall, hair pinned in a way that looked sensible rather than severe. She lifted the clipboard an inch, apology in the gesture. "Inspector Shaw asked if I would see whether you are free to pop back when you have a moment," she said. "No rush. He will speak to the family first."

Tessa glanced at the hatbox on the sideboard. The clamps held. The seam would not thank her for parading it. She nodded. "I will come."

"Thank you," the woman said. "He says he wants your eyes, not your opinion."

"Wise of him," Mabel murmured from her stool.

When the door was shut and quiet again, Tessa wrote a last line on her note and slid it into her pocket instead of under the glass.

If the floor tells one story and the rail tells another, which one lies.

Bramble hopped down and nosed the ribbon she had dropped that morning when the shop opened. He looked up at her as if to say the day would go where it wished regardless of knots.

"Keep watch," she told him. "And do not let anyone touch the hatbox."

He sat, then lifted one paw in solemn agreement, which was a trick for a biscuit and not a contract, but it felt like one all the same.

Outside, the village shifted again as people carried chairs into the light. The bells in the church tower marked the hour, clear and cool. Tessa locked the till, checked the clamps once more, and stepped out toward the hall with a head full of citrus and shine.

TWO

By noon, Fernvale had already shifted into its second version of the day. The garden behind the hall was filling with chairs for a ceremony that would not happen on time, the square had been swept twice for comfort, and The Thimble & Fern had become a holding bay for statements. Someone had pushed two tables together by the back window and brought out a plate of shortbread that no one touched. The fern wallpaper looked more serious in shadow.

Detective Inspector Malik Shaw had the knack of making a room steady. He did not bark; he set the pace the way a good metronome saves a piece from falling apart. He came to the counter where Tessa stood with Mabel and Bramble, took in the dog with a small nod, and kept his voice low.

"Thank you for coming," he said. "I would like your observations. Ground rules first."

He waited until she met his eye. She appreciated that. Rules went down better when they arrived as a contract rather than a lecture.

"You tell me what you saw, heard, or smelled, and what you did," he said. "No guessing, no filling gaps. If you remember detail later, you ring me. Do not test anything, move anything, or run your own experiments at the hall. Do not question other witnesses as if you wear my badge. You noticed useful things today, which is good. I prefer them to remain unspoiled by good intentions."

"I can manage that," Tessa said.

"Good. And we will keep this off village WhatsApp."

Mabel looked wounded. "I have never in my life put a fact on a thread."

"Mrs Clegg," Shaw said with a faint smile, "I have never in my life believed a village could keep a secret without inventing three more. Let us try anyway."

He gestured toward the back tables. Bramble chose a square of floor under the chair where Tessa would sit, circled once, and folded himself like a small rug. The light through the window turned the dust in the air to a fine gold. Tessa set her handbag on the floor, kept her notebook in her lap, and ran through the morning in order.

"The landing," Shaw prompted.

"Fresh polish," she said. "Shine like a mirror. A skid on the top landing before the first step. Not a scuff where a toe catches a stair edge, a slide where a shoe lost purchase on the flat."

"You touched it?"

"I looked along it. I did not put weight on it. I touched the newel cap. The varnish felt thin and slightly tacky. Not wet. As if a cleaner had lifted the finish."

"Cleaner."

She nodded. "A citrus note. Not sweet. Peel-forward."

"You are sensitive to solvents," he said without looking at his notes.

"Work hazard," she said. "I run a repair counter. Some cleaners smell alike; some announce themselves. This one does."

"The cup," he said. "You took it to your shop."

"It arrived wrong," she said. "The handle had been glued on the opposite side with a left-leaning set. The joint was bright and clean, no staining. Fresh. The same faint citrus hung around the cup when Isla opened the box. My own bottles were capped. I did not use a citrus solvent to reset. I used a neutral softener and a slow-cure adhesive. The handle is back where it belongs. I left it clamped on a shelf in the anteroom, out of reach."

Shaw tapped once on his pad with the end of his pencil. "You smelled the citrus at the cup and again at the rail."

"Yes."

"Did you see any cleaning bottles or wipes near the landing?"

"No. The caretaker was holding a mop when I arrived. Later, the caution sign appeared, but after, not before."

He wrote nothing for a moment. He had the look of a person matching notes to a mental grid. "Who touched the rail while you were there?"

"Len came past it. Poppy gripped it once, but lower. People avoided the cap because the paramedics were moving. I did not see Delia before they put the screen."

Shaw left a small space on his page, then closed the pad. "Thank you. That is clear. Now, I would like to speak to several people in turn. You will hear more than you need to. Do not engage unless I ask you to clarify a point. Today I am collecting maps rather than conclusions."

"Understood," Tessa said.

He raised a hand slightly. Poppy Hartley was waiting near the doorway, arms wrapped tight, a half-wilted posey clutched like a weapon. She came because she had nowhere else to put her fury.

Poppy sat. Her face had the glossy, fixed look of someone who has cried in a ladies' room and powdered over it. She glared at the untouched shortbread as if it had a nerve. "Can we get on with it," she said, then looked at Tessa. "No offence."

"None taken," Tessa said.

Shaw's tone did not change. "State your name for the record."

"Poppy Hartley. Sister of the bride and maid of honor, when people remember the honor part."

"Where were you at the time of the fall?"

"Rehearsing. I had ribbon to tame and a mother to settle and a florist who kept saying the word whimsical as if it was currency. I was in and out of the anteroom all morning. The tea table was my job. I can tell you the saucers were all in place at nine. I made a circle twice to check. I have a brain, you know."

"I do know," Shaw said. "Tell me about Delia."

"She ran things like a drill sergeant in silk," Poppy said. "Which is why we hired her." Her mouth pulled. "Past tense. She insisted on polishing for the pictures, told Len the sign was ugly, then said we needed the ivy banners higher. I never saw her on the landing after that. I was in the anteroom when someone shouted."

"Anyone ask you for the saucer?"

"Not then." Poppy shifted. "Later, at the hall, Isla said Tessa would bring the cup. I looked for the matching saucer to calm myself. Only, and this will cheer you, Inspector, I could not find it." She lifted her chin as if daring the room to call this trivial. "The saucer for the vintage cup was not on the table where I had put it, not in the crate, not in the box by the wall."

"Who else had their hands in the anteroom this morning?"

"Delia," Poppy said. "Florist. Len. Vera Locke, because she cannot keep herself out of any room where an invoice might be written. And my uncle Martin. He thinks he owns the hall because he is on the Trust."

Shaw let that settle. "We will come back to your uncle. When did you last see the saucer yourself?"

"Nine forty," Poppy said. "Blue stamp under the foot, little hairline on the rim. I remember because I argued with Delia about whether the flaw would show in a photograph. She said it would read as character."

"Did you move any boxes?" Shaw asked.

"I shifted the crate a foot and nearly died of lecture. Delia said nothing moves once placed."

"Did anyone mention a donation box?"

Poppy frowned. "Len muttered about clearing the storeroom and something going out to charity. That would have been before ten. He said the morning van was early. If he boxed anything from the anteroom by mistake, I will—" She clamped her mouth and looked at Tessa. "I will write a stern letter."

"Who knew about the cup and saucer being a set?" Shaw asked.

"Most of us," Poppy said. "Delia would not stop talking about cohesion. She planned the angles. The photographer would shoot the tea service from the right to catch the logo on the cake box and the printed napkins. The handle being wrong would ruin the symmetry. She said that, not me."

"Thank you," Shaw said. "You may wait in the lounge if you wish. Ask the desk for water."

Poppy stood, then halted. "I asked Delia for a favour last month," she said without prompting, as if the confession had been rehearsed. "I asked her to put a word in for me at the microloan office. I bake part time. I wanted a small oven upgrade to do cakes proper. She said she would not. Said she kept event lines clean. Said if she helped me at all, she would lose count of who wanted a handout. We had words. If someone tells you we had a row at last night's rehearsal, we did. We did not row this morning. Today was Isla's day. That is all."

Tessa watched her go, sharp with mixed feelings. People held anger the way they held teacups, for show or for warmth. Poppy had held both.

Len Porter came next. He looked as if someone had squeezed him like a soft fruit and left him on the stem. He perched, hands kneading his cap. His voice wrapped around apology like ivy around a post.

"I polish on Saturdays if there is a Sunday hire," he began without being asked. "It builds a base. I had the good wax, not the quick stuff, and I used the pad in circles, then buffed. I put the sign. I did. Then Delia said it spoiled the arrangement."

"The sign was not on the landing when the fall happened," Shaw said. "Who moved it, Mr Porter?"

"I did, to the side," Len said. "I meant to leave it visible. It was for the pictures, she said. I did not argue in front of the bride."

"Boxes," Shaw said. "Tell me about the boxes."

"The storeroom fills with nonsense," Len said, grateful to talk about anything with rules. "People bring donations for the jumble and think the hall is the jumble. Vases, plates, odd saucers. It was tight today, and Delia wanted the spare table in the anteroom. I shifted the old crate with china to the lobby for the charity van. I told Pete to come early. He did."

"Pete."

"Fernvale Community Barn," Len said. "They run pickups. Pete has a smile like a crack in ice and a clipboard that never matches the box. He came at nine twenty and took one crate and a bag. I marked it down, but I am not the one who logs, so no one will believe me. The book is in the drawer by the key hooks."

"Was the anteroom crate part of that collection?"

"No," Len said, affronted. "That was for today, not for charity. I only moved the storeroom lot."

"Anyone near the charity crate this morning?"

"Vera," Len said after a second's thought. "She gave me a speech about clutter making clients nervous. Said I should leave the hiring to professionals and the clearing to charities."

"Did you see her touch anything?"

"She prodded a saucer and said it was a shame to waste English bone on church sales," Len said. "It was one of those white ones from the council set. She did not pocket anything, Inspector. She would send a boy and a van for that."

Shaw's face did not register amusement. "Where were you when the fall occurred?"

"Back corridor," Len said. "Changing a bulb, moving a stepladder like a fool."

Tessa watched the way his hands turned his cap. Work had given him habits that did not fit a day like this. "Len," she said, because her voice carried less weight than Shaw's and more kindness, "when did you polish?"

"Half nine," he said. "Before the ribbons, after the chairs."

"And you used your usual wax."

"I made my own," he said, pride flirting with shame. "Beeswax and a sniff of lemon oil. It lifts the grain."

Shaw looked up. "Lemon oil."

"It is not harsh," Len said, defensive. "Smells better than turps."

"Did you wipe the rail with it?"

"No. I used a cloth," Len said. "Dust, not polish. The rail is varnished and fussy. You smear it and Mrs Dray from the women's institute writes a letter."

"Thank you," Shaw said. "You will stay available. And, Mr Porter, until I tell you, do not polish a thing."

"I would not dare," Len said, and meant it.

When Vera Locke arrived, the room shifted a notch. Vera always walked as if the air had been arranged for her height. She wore navy trousers, a crisp white shirt, and a thin gold bracelet that

25

clicked lightly against the table when she sat. Her hair was a sleek bob that looked vacuum sealed. She smelled like citrus and starch and the kind of warehouse that never admitted dust.

"Inspector," she said, poised. "I heard you wanted a statement. I have invoices to settle and a staff to pay, so I will keep it tidy."

Shaw did not rise to the hook. "State your name."

"Vera Locke, owner of Locke & Linen Hire. We supply to the hall most weeks, or did, until Delia decided she preferred to direct her own show. We collaborated on a few, then she went another way. That is business. I am sorry for your loss."

"Where were you at the time of the fall?"

"In the anteroom, then in the hall, then back to the van for a spare tablecloth because someone had not measured their trestle correctly," she said, a quick glance toward the ceiling for patience. "I did not see her fall. I heard the shout. I am sorry. It was ugly."

"Did you go up on the landing this morning?"

"Yes. Twice. Once to check the sightlines for the banner and once to tell Len to move the sign because it spoiled the photographs. You will hear that as if it was a crime. It was common sense. I do not polish. I employ people for that. I have a reputation to maintain and slipping clients are bad for business."

"What did you bring into the hall today?" Shaw asked.

"Tablecloths, napkins, two white cake stands, a set of plain saucers and teacups to supplement the vintage set, and a crate of ribbon spares. I sourced the best price on the linen, as always."

"Did you handle any of the vintage china?"

"I touched nothing from the family," she said. "I am not a fool."

"Did you speak to Mr Porter about donations?"

"I told him to empty the storeroom before someone broke an ankle and sued my insurance," she said without heat. "He said the Barn van was coming. I said good and moved on with my day."

"Did you donate anything yourself this morning?" Shaw asked.

"My warehouse clears on Tuesdays," she said. "Today is Saturday. I sent a crate of offcuts to the school last night for bunting. If a driver of mine delivered to charity this morning I will expect to see it on my log with a signature. You may too."

Tessa did not move. Vera had brought the scent with her, clean and pointed. It clung to her cuffs and her hands, a hint of something that cut varnish if used on the wrong surface. Vera's bracelet clicked once more as she folded her hands.

"Tell me about Delia," Shaw said.

"We were capable of being in a room together," Vera said. "That is the kindest way to phrase it. She liked to control every ribbon and every breath. She had taken the Fernvale account, which had formerly been mine. She said she wanted a fresh look. She meant my invoices offended her. She ran a very pretty show. She did not pay market rates to suppliers."

"Did you argue with her this week?"

"We spoke yesterday about chair spacing," Vera said. "If anyone heard raised voices, they heard mine. I said a meter means a meter and not a meter minus a vase. She informed me she could do maths. I congratulated her. That is the extent."

"Your cleaning kit," Shaw said. "What do you use on hires?"

"Microfibre and a mild citrus wipe for sticky hands," she said. "We do not strip varnish. We remove fingerprints. If your man tells you lemon oil can lift a finish, he is right. We did not use it."

"What brand of wipe?" He sounded indifferent. He never was.

"The good brand," she said, and smiled in a way that tried to control the frame. "I am sure you can read packaging as well as an invoice."

Shaw did not bite. "Thank you, Ms Locke. You may wait outside."

She stood, gave Tessa the briefest glance that acknowledged expertise without conceding ground, and left in a thread of citrus and starch. Mabel breathed out when the door shut.

"If packing judgement came in tins," Mabel said, "she would sell out by lunch."

"Do not underestimate judgement in a day job," Tessa said.

Martin Hale did not bother with the desk. He was on his phone when he arrived, ended the call with a polished thank you, and tucked the device away as if it were a pocket square. He sat like a man accustomed to committees and polished floors. His hair had an expensive sort of grey.

"Detective Inspector," he said. "I have been with my nephew and his bride. We are trying to manage the shock."

Shaw nodded. "State your name and your position for the record."

"Martin Hale, Laurel Trust trustee, uncle to the groom, and procurement chair for the hall refurbishments. I do not draw a salary. I shepherd projects."

"Where were you at the time of the fall?"

"In the anteroom, then the garden," he said. "I spoke briefly to Ms Locke about the table sizes. I took a call from the caterer on the far side of the hall because the reception was poor, then stepped outside to confirm vehicle access through Canal Gate. The next thing I heard was shouting."

"Did you move any signs or furnishings on the landing?"

"I did not," he said. "I told Len to keep the corridor clear. I did not question Delia's taste. I learnt long ago to leave placement to the people who care about chairs."

"Did you handle vintage china this morning?"

"No. I carry insurance for many things in life, Inspector. Replacing a family heirloom is not one."

"Mr Hale," Shaw said, "did the hall send a donation crate to charity this morning?"

"The hall does not," Martin said, mild. "Mr Porter might, because he acts as if the storeroom is his to curate. The Trust intends to formalise procedures. I have a procurement plan in draft."

"Who signs off on gifts to the charity barn?"

"At present, no one. We rely on the good sense of staff and volunteers," Martin said. "Which, as you will point out, is sloppy. Write it down, Inspector. I will concede it."

"Did you speak to Ms Hartley's sister this morning?"

"I did," he said. "Poppy was fine on the details and poor on delegation. I redirected her attention to tasks that did not involve climbing on chairs. I also reminded her that the hall is a shared space and not her personal workshop."

"Did you speak to Delia?"

"Of course. We spoke about the order of processional because she wanted the bride to drift in as the doors opened. I advised against lingering under the arch. The door sticks. She had a clipboard. I deferred. We managed as we always do, Inspector. I said strong words about budgets last month and we all lived to speak again."

"Mr Hale," Shaw said, tone as level as a spirit level, "did you possess or control any duplicate keys to the hall that are not on the registry?"

Martin smiled in a way that said he recognised a probe and admired the blade. "We keep spare sets. They are signed in and out by the office. If a duplicate lurks, it lurks in the same shadows as every village duplicate since keys were invented. If you ask me whether I did a run to the locksmith last week, I did not. We have enough metal on hooks to collar a herd."

"Did you go near the landing rail this morning?"

"I passed it," he said. "I did not stroke it. If you found oils on the cap, they are not mine."

"Did you see Ms Locke on the landing?"

"Yes. She told Len to move the sign and he moved it. He did not like it. He does as he is told when someone wears a shirt with a pressed seam."

"Last question for now," Shaw said. "Were you aware that

the matching saucer to a vintage teacup is missing from the anteroom?"

Martin blinked once. "I was not. I am now. I expect it will turn up in a box under a vase, as all lost things do in rooms run by amateurs."

"Thank you," Shaw said. "Do not leave town."

Martin did not dignify that with an answer. He rose, nodded to Mabel as if to a committee member he needed later, and left without checking his phone, which was discipline if nothing else.

Shaw kept the room moving. He took statements from the florist, the photographer's assistant, and the boy on the bicycle who had shouted through Ink & Ivy's window. He took a few quiet minutes between each, standing with his pencil in hand and his eyes on nothing, the way a person lets thoughts line up.

When he called Tessa back for a second round, it was not to ask for new facts but to place hers. "Your nose may be useful," he said, and left it at that.

She turned her notebook to a fresh page. "You will want to know that Vera's cuffs carry the same peel note," she said, careful to mark it as observation, not accusation. "Her bracelet too."

"And Len uses lemon oil in his wax," Shaw said. "The rail had a faint dull patch, as you said. If someone wiped it with a stronger citrus product, we will know when the lab cuts the residue. Today we are still at the stage where people say, I meant well."

"The saucer," Tessa said. "Poppy lost it between nine forty and eleven. Len sent a donation crate out at nine twenty with Pete from the Barn. Vera prodded china in the lobby and told Len to stop tripping over it. Those facts stand next to one another without shaking hands."

"They will shake hands later if they wish," Shaw said. "I will send a car to Fernvale Community Barn. If a saucer went with that crate, we will have a log, a signature, or a shrug."

"Pete does love a shrug," Mabel said from her chair. "He once signed a piano in as a lamp."

"Thank you," Shaw said dryly. "I will prepare myself."

A young constable stuck his head in from the corridor. "Sir. Family need an update. And, the charity barn says their van was redirected to a church sale pick-up in Broadoak after nine. They made it back to Fernvale at ten fifty-five, but the crate from the hall had already been signed into their back room by a volunteer. No one remembers who carried it in."

"Of course no one remembers," Shaw said in a tone that did not blame the constable. "Get names. We will go ourselves."

The constable nodded and vanished.

Shaw closed his notebook. "Ms Harper, I prefer witness statements before gossip grows teeth. You gave me a clean one. Do you intend to keep watch, or to involve yourself?"

"I intend to see what is in front of me," she said. "I will not touch your rail."

"Good," he said. "If you notice something, tell me. If you invent something to fill the quiet, tell Mabel. She will check you."

"I check everyone," Mabel said. "Even myself."

Shaw let that stand as reassurance and warning both. He stood. "Stretch your legs. Go home if you need to sit with your kettle. We will reach out for formalities."

Tessa rose. Bramble rose. The Thimble & Fern breathed in and out as the wedding guests who had become witnesses filtered back toward the hall and the garden where chairs waited as if patience could serve as a prayer.

On their way to the door, a whisper from the bar caught and lingered, because village whispers did not know how to keep their volume down. "They say the matching saucer turned up at the Barn," someone said. "In a donation box. Logged by Gwen in the back room."

"Logged when," another voice asked.

"Before the ambulance," the whisperer said, with that fragile pride of a person who gets to be first. "Which means it went out before she fell."

Tessa felt the words land and take a seat in her mind where they would not be knocked over: before the ambulance, which meant before the fall. She did not look toward the bar and she did not ask for clarity. She went outside, where the sky had decided to keep up appearances.

Bramble steered her the way dogs lead people who think they are leading dogs. He took her back toward Ivy Lane by the longer route, the one that passed the green and the notice board with the flyer for the Laurel Trust's Autumn Gala pinned square with brass tacks. On the bottom corner of the flyer, someone had written in small, neat letters, Too dear for local pockets. Someone else had underlined dear twice.

Mabel matched her stride. "Your face," she said. "I know that face. It holds a piece and stares at the space where the next piece lives."

"I do not like the saucer in a charity crate before a fall on a polished landing," Tessa said. "It puts the morning in two boxes."

"You want to lay eyes on the Barn," Mabel said. "I do too. The last time I donated there, I received three stickers and a lecture about fire exits."

"Shaw is already on it," Tessa said. "He will prefer my eyes not to tromp through his footprints."

"We can tromp around the footprints," Mabel said. "From the front of the counter, with our hands in our pockets, like citizens."

Tessa smiled without meaning to. "You have a genius for lawful mischief."

"Age helps," Mabel said. "Everyone assumes my eyebrows are harmless."

They did not go to the Barn. They went back to Ink & Ivy. The hatbox sat high on the shelf where she had left it; the clamps held faithful as a hymn. She checked the seam with a mirror rather than fingers. The line was clean. The angle sat at ease. She felt a small, useful lift at the sight. It is a relief to set one thing to rights when the rest will not oblige.

The bell chimed. The young constable came in with a polite hat in his hand and a careful step that did not cross thresholds he did not know. "Ms Harper," he said. "Inspector Shaw would like to borrow you for twenty minutes for a walk to the Barn." He glanced at Bramble and then at the floor. "The dog can come if he behaves."

"Bramble has a strict code," Mabel said. "He never misbehaves within sight of authority."

"Good," the constable said gravely. "We will keep him in sight."

The Fernvale Community Barn lived in a long brick that used to smell of apples and now smelled of the twentieth century in cardboard. A painted sign with a crooked heart announced OPEN and two women in aprons manned a counter where bric-a-brac arrived with optimism and left with stories. Behind them, rows of shelves ran with plates and lamps and books that had meant the world to someone once.

Shaw was already there, flipping through a log with the patience of a person who had once learned to read sideways. He nodded to Tessa, then to Bramble, who treated the Barn with the respect due to a cathedral of smells.

"Gwen signed in the hall crate at nine forty-seven," Shaw said without preface. "She says Pete from the Barn is reliable when his kettle is on and vague when it is not."

Gwen herself, a woman with clipped hair and two pens in her apron, shrugged at this with good cheer. "I put the crate there," she said, pointing to a space on the floor near the receiving desk. "Then I moved it to the back room because the front was full of lamps. There was a saucer on top. I remember because it had a blue stamp and a little hairline. I said to myself, Ruth will want to price that as a set if she can find the cup, then I thought, who donates single saucers, and then a man came in with a box of train magazines and I forgot."

"Who else touched the crate?" Shaw asked.

"Dorothy carried it with me," Gwen said. "She will tell you the same. We did not rifle it. We do not have time to rifle, Inspector. People give us their attics every Saturday and take home a vase."

"Did anyone come in from the hall after ten to ask for a saucer?" Shaw asked.

"No," Gwen said. "We had two browsers looking for a jug, a man who wanted to argue about whether this is antique" — she gestured at a jug that was bravely doing its best — "and a woman who needed a lamp with a plug and a personality. No brides. No planners. I am sorry about your news. Delia bought a rug from us once and haggled for thirty minutes as if we were the Ritz."

Shaw nodded. "May we see the crate."

Gwen led them to the back room, where a neat stack of Saturday had lined up behind a table with a cash tin. The hall crate sat against the wall. Someone had written HALL MIXED on the side in felt tip. On top lay a saucer with a blue stamp under the foot and a fine line along the rim. It had that look some old white has, as if it glowed from within.

Poppy's description had been exact. Tessa looked but did not touch. The hairline ran from two o'clock to four, clean and old. There were no tea stains on the surface, only a shadow where a cup had sat many mornings. She leaned closer. Near the notch where the cup's foot had rested, a faint half-moon of varnish glimmered, so fine she might have missed it if not for the light. No, not varnish, not shine. A clear smear where something had kissed the edge. She did not say the word in her head. She took one step back.

Shaw watched her face. "We will bag it," he said to the constable. "Photograph, then lift. Print the crate handle. Photograph the top layer. I want an image of that smear."

Gwen bristled. "We can price around police work, Inspector, but please do not turn my back room into a lab forever. The church sale men will arrive at four with folding tables and opinions."

"It will be neat when we leave," Shaw said.

"Hold him to that," Mabel told Gwen. "He makes promises like a person who intends to keep them."

"Rare," Gwen said, appeased.

Shaw turned to Tessa. "This helps us place time. If the saucer entered the Barn before the fall, then someone moved part of a set out of the hall when the set was still meant to be complete. Either careless or deliberate."

"Or convenient," Tessa said. "If the saucer did not match the plan, off it went. People tidy accidents after they happen. They also tidy before."

He gave her one of those flicker looks that acknowledged a point without giving ground. "Do you know why a person would send a single saucer to charity on a wedding morning?"

"Impulse," Tessa said. "Or a plan that required the cup to look odd and the saucer to be elsewhere."

Mabel made a small sound. "Child."

Tessa glanced down. Bramble had found a corner where a faint smell of biscuits had lodged and was breathing it in with the seriousness of a scholar. He looked up at her, pleased to be included in a day that offered purpose and crumbs.

Shaw folded his notebook. "We will take the saucer and the crate for a day," he said to Gwen. "We will bring them back if they do not turn into evidence."

"If they turn into evidence," Gwen said stoutly, "we want a sign explaining why the charity has an empty shelf."

"You will have one," Shaw said.

On the way out, Ruth at the counter tapped the log with a nail. "Inspector," she said. "If that saucer matters, please note the time we wrote. Gwen wrote nine forty-seven because she signed the ledger after she'd had her tea, which was late. Pete dropped the crate on the floor at nine twenty-eight. He knocked the bell.

I remember because it scared the life out of Dot. She dropped a candlestick on her foot and swore like a person who has met a candlestick before."

Shaw amended the time, then thanked her. Outside, the day had warmed by a degree that felt like a courtesy. Mabel shaded her eyes with her hand and squinted toward the hall spire. The village was still busy in a quiet way. The idea of tea had become a duty rather than a pleasure.

"Ms Harper," Shaw said, walking back toward the green at a pace that matched a mind in gear. "You will hear things before I do because people think you hear without writing. That is a gift. Be careful with it."

"I will not tangle your lines," she said. "And I will bring you anything I cannot put down."

"Good," he said. "Tell me one thing before we part. Why did you study the handle as if it had a mind of its own."

"Because whoever set it did not ask a hand what it likes," she said. "A left-dominant set on a cup chosen for a right-leaning photograph is a conflict, not an error. It draws the eye. It invites comment. It makes the cup perform rather than sit."

"And the saucer," he said.

"Made the pair complete or incomplete on command," she said. "A set is a story. Remove one piece and you write a new paragraph."

He almost smiled. "Try not to write my report."

"I would never," she said. "Your handwriting is legible."

Mabel snorted. Bramble frog-marched a pigeon away from a sandwich wrapper and looked pleased with himself. They reached Ivy Lane without deciding to, the way feet go to the known when the mind is working.

At Ink & Ivy, the air held the warm paper scent that made sense of days. Tessa put the kettle on and lined three mugs on the counter. She stood with both hands around her own tea and watched the steam. The morning had offered three small anchors. Citrus on a rail. Citrus on a cup. A saucer that left before anyone fell. None of those things were grief or motive. They were shapes.

Mabel sipped and made a face at the strength. "You will not sleep tonight."

"I will sleep," Tessa said. "Eventually. I do not thrive on caffeine, I survive it."

"Better than thriving on gossip," Mabel said. She set her mug down. "We will see Vera again before this is done."

"We will see all of them," Tessa said. "Poppy, Len, Vera, Martin. And the person we have not named yet because every room has one."

Mabel nodded. "The one who knows where the light switch lives."

"Or the one who practices in the dark," Tessa said.

Bramble thumped his tail twice, then went to sit under the shelf where the hatbox rested, as if he had elected himself guardian of porcelain. Tessa wrote three precise lines in her notebook and closed it before the page grew chatty.

Skid before stair. Citrus on rail and cup. Saucer signed into Barn at 9:28.

She underlined the time once and circled it. Then she opened the shop door, let the bell chime, and allowed the day to go on pretending to be normal while it quietly stacked its clues.

THREE

By mid afternoon the hall wore a quieter face. The ambulance lights were gone. The police tape did not shout, it simply wrapped the landing like ribbon with purpose. In the garden, the family had done what families do. They had found chairs and a priest and a way to say something steady about a woman who did not deserve an abrupt ending. The urns of lavender looked braver in the sun than they had under the cornice.

Detective Inspector Shaw had granted Tessa a short visit under escort to collect her clamps and the hatbox. He had said, in that level way of his, that she could walk the route once with Len Porter and put her eyes on the places she had already looked at this morning. No touching, no testing. Observe and go.

Mabel came along because she did not believe in sending anyone into a pool of grief without a second towel. Bramble came because he had decided he worked here now.

Len met them at the door with a sort of stiff humility. He had put on a clean shirt. He held his cap. He had not shaved because nobody shaves between disasters. "Inspector says you can come in," he said. "Only the landing is marked. You may step round if you mind your feet."

"We will mind our feet," Tessa said.

The smell at the lobby was polish and stone and something else tucked away behind a door. Len's closet of a store cupboard stood open for once. Inside, on the floor, sat a galvanised bucket with a waxy sheen at the rim. A mop leaned against the wall, its strands flattened from recent use. On the shelf above, tins lived in rows like well-behaved pupils. Some had labels. Some did not. A small stack of soft cloths waited, folded, and a brush hung by its wire as if ashamed.

Len flushed when he saw her look. "You will say that is careless," he said. "The bucket. I should empty and stack, I know."

"I will say it looks like work," Tessa said. "What is in the bucket."

"My blend," he said, pride and guilt at war. "Beeswax grated and warmed with a drop of lemon oil and white spirit. The spirit off gasses, the wax sets, and then you buff. Makes the floor speak when light hits it. Delia asked for shine. I gave shine."

Mabel peered into the bucket with a frown that was more curious than cross. "How many drops make a drop."

"Two," he said. "Sometimes three if the wax is stubborn."

"And your mop," Tessa said. "You used the bucket for the mop as well as the pad."

"I use the mop to spread, pad to buff," he said. "Old habit. The pad is cleaner than my hands most days."

She looked at the mop head. The strands carried a faint tack.

She did not touch, but she felt the way a person feels weather through a window. A residue had settled here and there in the fringe, as if it had kissed the floor and kept a trace. The smell in the cupboard was beeswax, lemon, and paraffin, the sort of scent you might call honest if you had never met a banister that did not wish to be lifted.

"Where did you mix it," she asked.

"Here," he said, then winced. "Inspector will tell me to mix outside. I know. It was early and I was in a hurry and the garden smelled like cut grass and I felt righteous."

"Righteous is not a crime," Mabel said.

"Today anything could be," he said, low.

They moved to the corridor. The mop marks showed themselves if you knew how to read them. Circles where a pad had turned. Long strokes where a handle had travelled. The pattern on the top landing formed an open spiral that stopped three hand spans from the newel. He had not buffed right to the edge. Either time had run out or Len's instinct had declared that shine at a drop does not need a mirror.

Tessa crouched, careful. The skid mark she had seen earlier was now marked with a small numbered tent. It cut across the spiral like a diagonal pencil line through a plate of glass. If she set the skid against the buffer's path, the story on the floor ran counter to the story in the bucket. She kept that to herself. It was for Shaw's pencil, not her tongue.

Len stood with his cap crushed in his hands. "It looks bad," he said. "I am not blind."

"It looks like a floor that had a job," she said. "It does not look like intent."

"Tell that to Poppy," he said, bleak. "She called me a murderer under her breath. Then she cried and apologised and called me a fool instead. It is hard to tell which is worse."

"Fool is better," Mabel said. "Fool leaves tomorrow open."

He led them past the tape to the anteroom. Someone had placed the hatbox on the top shelf as Tessa had asked. The clamps still held. She checked the seam with the mirror she kept for angles. The line was calm and true. The handle sat in the right place and gave nothing away. She decided it could travel. She lowered the clamps with the tenderness of a person easing a baby's arm into a cardigan and set the cup back in its nest.

"Thank you," Isla's mother said from the doorway, her voice hushed and even. "We are doing the best parts we can."

"You are doing very well," Mabel said. "Tea is heavy and you are carrying several kettles."

The woman's mouth softened. She nodded and left them to it.

They followed Len along the back corridor to his office. It was a little room with a high window, a desk that wanted to be bigger, and a wall where keys lived on hooks like roosting birds. Above the hooks, wooden labels showed their fussy handwriting: Main, Side, Boiler, Office, Canal Gate, Spare, Spare B, Back Corridor, Store, Lift. Some had two copies hanging. Some had one.

On the far right, two hooks were bare. One label read Back Corridor. The metal screw below was empty and showed a half-moon of cleaner shine where a fob had swung and knocked. The second label read Spare B. Below it, dust marked the outline of a small shape that looked, to an attentive eye, like a teapot. Not a drawing, only a silhouette where dust had shaded around a keyring that was no longer there.

Tessa stood as if considering the overall effect. She did not point. She did not reach. She let the image sit with her. A novelty fob had lived there long enough to make its own shadow. It did not live there now.

Len saw where her eyes rested and grimaced. "Before you ask," he said, "Spare B walks. The volunteer choir borrows it for Thursday practice and forgets to bring it back. The bell ringers take it and return it with a biscuit tied to it. The drama group sign it out three nights in a row and then insist they never had it.

I have shouted. I have written. I have thought about a nail gun."

"Does Spare B usually wear a teapot," Tessa asked, mild.

"It did," he said. "We have a tray of novelty fobs Mrs Dray bought for fundraising. Little tin teapots and spoons and a trumpet. People swap them round because they cannot tell their keys without a hat on. If you want them to notice a hook is empty, give the hook a silly hat."

"Who last signed it out," Mabel asked.

Len pulled a ledger from the drawer under the hooks. It was ruled and stamped and mostly empty of discipline. Names trooped across the page in a procession of hands. The choir, the church flower ladies, the Laurel Trust, the Fernvale Players, the WI, the Craft Fayre Committee. A few entries were crisp with office pen. A few were hopeful pencil smudges. One month had been surrendered entirely to the Harvest Fair, which had sent keys out with the urgency of a drought.

Len ran his finger down this week. "Thursday," he said. "Fernvale Players, hall stage door. Friday, Trust office, Martin Hale, Canal Gate. Spare B shows a line but no name. I shouted about that at nine, then went to fetch my pad. When I came back, someone had written in Vera's neatness, Locke & Linen, anteroom, return by noon. I do not like it when people fix my book for me."

Tessa did not blink. She did not love coincidences either. "You are sure it was her hand."

"I am old enough to know a tidy signature when I meet one," he said. "She writes like a ruler."

"Did she return it by noon," Mabel asked.

"She returned a key," Len said. "I did not check the fob because I had a landing to make and a planner in my ear. At eleven thirty I had a spare set in my pocket. I was not counting teapots."

Tessa leaned in to look at the hook again without leaning in at all. The dust outline wore the rounded lid of a tiny pot. The screw shone brighter at the top where it had polished under weight. She filed the picture where she kept angles and joins.

"Back Corridor," she said, nodding toward the other empty hook. "Who had that."

Len grimaced again. "Me," he said. "I moved it to my belt when I set up the stepladder. Then I gave it to Delia when she snapped her fingers. Not this morning. Yesterday. She had a checklist and gave me the line about delays. She wanted the back corridor clear for a reveal. She meant a door that opens on cue. I like a reveal as much as the next person. I also like working hinges."

"Does the Back Corridor key live on a novelty fob as well," Tessa asked.

"It used to," he said. "A trumpet. The trumpet went home with Mr Pratt from the brass band and came back two years later with a dent. The key did not come back with it. I had duplicates cut and put them all on boring rings. Everyone complained and then forgot."

"What about Canal Gate," Mabel asked, because Mabel knew when a word round a village deserved a poke. "Who had that this week."

"Martin," Len said. "He likes to walk suppliers through and tell them stories about funding. He holds the gate high as if it is generous. I imagine he believes it is."

He set the ledger down and moved a little tin from one side of his desk to the other. The tin had the faded picture of a seaside on the lid. He opened it and revealed coins and folded notes in a mess that would have made a tax man itch. He shut it again with a small clack and did not look at them as if perhaps they would take the hint and vanish.

"I do odd jobs," he said to the tin rather than to them. "Cash. The sort of things the hall does not invoice because no one would pay for the line item. I water the back pots when Mrs Dray forgets. I swap a bulb in the boileroom. I sand a splinter on a chair no one else will love. People give me a fiver and say I am a star and I put it in a tin and then at Christmas I buy biscuits for the staff. I declare what I should declare on paper. I am not a thief."

Tessa raised her hands, palms empty. "We came to look at wax and hooks. Not your soul."

"My soul is attached to the hooks," he said. "Today it feels nailed there."

"Len," Mabel said, softer, "who asked you to polish this morning. Truly."

He looked at the bucket in his head and searched for a different word than pride. "Delia," he said. "She came in early with a bundle of ribbon and said the landing needed to glow. She said the camera would love it. I said it would be slippery until it buffed. She said she would put the sign. I put the sign. We moved it to the side and then we moved it further because it spoiled the line of the shot."

"Who moved it further," Tessa asked.

"Me," he said. "At Vera's direction. She speaks like a budget. People obey."

He scrubbed a hand over his face. "I do cash jobs," he went on, as if ripping off a plaster. "I take money to run a buffer round the village hall's side rooms when the toddlers spill juice. I earned twenty quid yesterday waxing the anteroom for the tea. People will say I wanted this level of shine. They will say I chased it. I did not want this shine."

Tessa nodded. "We are allowed to despise outcomes we did not intend."

"And we are allowed to admit when they were avoidable," he said. "I am not thick."

"No," she said. "You are a man who mixed beeswax inside on a hot morning and let a planner move a sign."

"And a woman fell," he said.

They stood together in the small office with the weight of that in the corners. Outside, a child's laugh from the green came in through the high window and made the room feel smaller. Bramble put his chin on Len's shoe in a gesture that pretended to be casual and was not.

When Shaw stepped in, he did not fill the doorway. He kept the hall's tone even. He looked at the keys and then at Tessa and then at Len's face. He said, "How are we doing," in a way that was not about progress.

"Collecting clamps," Tessa said. "Len is showing us how keys live."

"Keys," Shaw said. "They grow like ivy and then disappear like mist."

He went to the hooks and ran a finger under the labels rather than over the metal. "Back Corridor empty. Spare B empty," he said. "Mr Porter, you will give me a list of all duplicates for all entries within the hour. If anyone has a second cut that is not on this board, I want their name."

"It will be a long list," Len warned.

"Make it longer," Shaw said. "If you leave out anyone you think would be offended, I will put them back in with notes about their offence."

Mabel approved of this. "That is the correct order," she said.

Shaw's gaze rested on the dust outline and moved on, which is the same as saying it did not move on at all. "Ms Harper," he said, "clamps in hand and then fresh air. We will take your witness statement addendum later. Mr Porter, the wax bucket stays where it is until my scenes of crime officer has lifted samples. The mop stays. Everything stays. If the cleaner in there lifts varnish, I will hear it sing in a lab."

"Understood," Len said. "Do I go home or stand in a corner until someone points."

"You go to your chair in the office and make your list," Shaw said. "If you stand in a corner, Mrs Dray will find you and feed you resentment."

Len huffed what might have been a laugh. "She has a pantry full."

Shaw nodded to Tessa. "Thank you for your patience," he said.

"And for returning my tape to me as if it belonged to you."

"It looked lost," she said.

He left them to collect the hatbox. On the way back through the lobby, Tessa paused by the community notice board. The collage of Fernvale life always made her smile. Posters for yoga and bell ringing and a call for volunteers to man the Canal Gate during the autumn gala. Someone had pinned a glossy photograph from the Spring Fete. It showed a line of raffle prizes on a table. One of the prizes was a little tin keyring in the shape of a teapot, tied with a ribbon as if dressing for a party. Another photograph, half covered by a flier, showed a group of committee members at the same table. She could not see faces clearly. The teapot shape was clear enough.

She did not take the photograph down. She did not lift the flier. She stood still and let her eyes do their work. The shape on the hook upstairs matched the shape on the raffle table. Teapot fobs had made their way into every pocket in Fernvale. That was the point of a fundraiser. Everyone leaves with a hat for a key.

"Ready," Mabel said, gentle.

"Ready," Tessa said.

Bramble took the lead out of habit and pride. On the path to Ivy Lane, the village looked like itself again, which was the trick villages learn. A woman on a bicycle rang her bell for no reason other than the joy of ringing. A man at the bakery chose a bun with intent as if this decision required his best self. Life holds grief and pastry with the same hand.

Back at Ink & Ivy, the quiet let Tessa hear what her head had not heard inside the hall. She set the hatbox on the counter and opened it. The handle looked back at her like a friend returned from a small trouble. She let herself feel a brief pulse of relief that a thing she could fix had been fixed.

Mabel filled the kettle. "Your face again," she said, warm rather than teasing. "You have a row of notes queuing."

Tessa took out her notebook and wrote without commentary.

Len's bucket: beeswax, lemon oil, white spirit. Mop head tacky. Spiral buff stops short of newel. Skid cuts across spiral.

Office: key board. Back Corridor hook empty. Spare B hook empty. Dust outline teapot fob on Spare B. Ledger: Spare B blank at 9, later filled in neat hand as Locke & Linen. Back Corridor to Delia yesterday. Canal Gate to Martin Friday.

Cash tin in drawer. Len admits cash jobs, side polish. Not a villain. Not today.

She added, underlined once: Notice board Spring Fete photo. Tin teapot fobs given as prizes. Shape match.

Mabel set a mug by her elbow and read the lines upside down because Mabel had once taught children to read upside down and never lost the knack. "All true," she said. "Now give yourself one line for what you are not sure about."

Tessa hesitated, then wrote: Citrus on rail not same as Len's wax. Possible wipe.

She closed the book and rested her hands on it for a moment. "There is a world where that landing would still have been slippery without anyone's help," she said. "And a second world where a hand slid because something lifted the varnish. We are standing in the doorway between."

"Then let the man with the pencil measure the doorway," Mabel said. "You have done your bit."

"I know," Tessa said. "I cannot walk past a hook with a shadow and pretend I have not seen it."

"No one asked you to pretend," Mabel said. "We asked you not to pocket evidence and you behaved like a saint."

Bramble decided this was a moment for a biscuit. Tessa obliged. He crunched with a seriousness that always charmed her. He went to sit under the shelf where the hatbox lived and looked, for all the world, like a sentry who had taken vows.

The bell chimed. Vera Locke appeared, her bob faultless, her expression arranged for sympathy. She had a bag over her shoulder with her logo stitched on in white. Citrus walked in with her, clean and professional.

"I am here to settle an invoice," she said to Tessa with a smile that put money where grief had been. "Events do not stop because the worst happens. The hall must be in order."

Mabel did not smile back. "Inspector Shaw is still in the building," she said. "You may wish to run your philosophy past him."

"I already have," Vera said. "He prefers receipts to opinions."

"We are close friends with receipts," Tessa said, and wrote a neat line on the top page of her pad that read Locke present at 15:42, citrus noted.

Vera glanced at the hatbox. "You are a marvel," she said. "Brides need marvellous people. I hope you used an adhesive that respects porcelain."

"I did," Tessa said. "We are all trying to respect porcelain today."

Vera's look acknowledged the double meaning and declined to sit with it. She took a business card from her bag and set it on the counter. "If you ever want to expand to event repairs," she said, pleasant, "I hire clever hands."

"I am content as I am," Tessa said.

"Few can say that," Vera replied. She left with the same ghost of citrus.

Mabel exhaled. "She writes like a ruler and speaks like a balance sheet," she said. "I cannot fault either and yet my skin itches."

"Keep the itch," Tessa said. "It will remind us to wash our hands."

She turned the business card over. On the back, in that neat, rulered hand, someone had written, Spare set returned, 11:55. The date was today. There was a dot where a person who likes neatness had allowed themselves a tiny flourish.

Tessa put the card under the counter glass beside her note about the teapot silhouette. She would show both to Shaw. She would ask him whether the wipe in Vera's kit sang the same peel note as the rail. She would ask him about the ledger entry and the late neatness.

For now she wrote one more line in her book.

Hooks tell stories. So do gaps.

Then she closed the cover and reached for the kettle again, because it was four o'clock and that is what you do in a village when the air has been strained through grief. You put water on to boil and you wait for the next knock on the door.

FOUR

Vera Locke's warehouse lived on the edge of Fernvale where the old brick backs onto the canal path. The sign over the roller door read Locke & Linen Hire in a font that looked like a contract. Inside, light fell in pale sheets from high windows onto neat aisles of crates. Everything was labelled. Everything had a place. The air held starch, cotton, a faint metallic hum from a plug bank, and a bright peel scent that pinged the back of Tessa's nose.

A woman at the front desk checked a clipboard and did not bother with small talk. "Ms Locke is expecting you," she said. "Straight along, last bay on the right."

Mabel walked at Tessa's side with the air of a person who had once been a librarian and still believed in the moral power of labels. Bramble trotted closer than usual. Concrete floors and pallet jacks demand sensible paws.

Vera stood at a long steel bench like a doctor at a theatre. Her shirt sleeves were rolled with crisp precision. On the bench lay a half built prop arch wrapped in silk ivy, a tray of ribbon spools, a box of napkin rings, and a little aluminium heat gun resting on a silicone mat. A tool caddy sat to one side. Its compartments held bottles and tubes and packets in three strict rows: adhesives, removers, cloths.

"You came for an invoice," Vera said, letting the words do two jobs. "Stay for a tour. Most people do not care how the sausage is made. I prefer clients who respect process."

"I prefer to see the thing you sell," Tessa said. "It helps when people insist on results without understanding why their choices wobble."

Vera's mouth tipped a fraction, approval without warmth. "Quite," she said. She tapped the caddy. "This is the kit my team carries to sites. I rotate stock weekly and record usage daily. If anyone uses more than allowance, I know where they were and what they touched."

"Your kit smells like peel," Mabel observed.

"It smells like performance," Vera replied. "Citrus cuts finger grease, lipstick, candle soot. It leaves the linen as if hands had never gone near it."

Tessa let her eyes map the caddy. Three bottle sizes ran left to right. The smallest row held single-use wipes in matte white packets, the kind that live in every event bag for emergencies. The mid row held clear bottles with tamper rings and printed hazard diamonds, decanted and labelled in a tidy hand: Neutral Remover No. 2, Citrus Remover No. 12, Protein Lift. The largest row held gel adhesives in silver tubes and two-part epoxy in small paired syringes. None of it looked slapdash. All of it suggested control.

She lifted a brow, not a hand. "Walk me through your favourites," she said, as if asking a baker about flour.

Vera obliged because this was her element. "Gel for fast fixes on non porous surfaces," she said, tapping a tube. "Solvent based for ribbon hardware. Two part epoxy for weight and for things no one honest should do on a Saturday. The neutral remover lifts general grime without harming finishes. Citrus No. 12 lifts tape residue and human oils quickly. Protein Lift does lipstick and tea. We do not strip varnish. We return sheen."

"Citrus No. 12," Tessa repeated, mild. The number sat like a neat stitch. "Different from the lemon oil everyone keeps under the sink."

"Lemon oil is furniture perfume," Vera said. "It feeds wood in private homes. On site I require speed and predictability. No smearing, no bloom, no residue you can see in a flash photograph. No. 12 evaporates clean. It is not cheap. It is also the only thing I have used in three years that does the job on a varnished rail without leaving drag."

Mabel sent Tessa a small look. Peel, rail, drag. Tessa wrote the words in her head, then set them on a mental shelf next to the newel cap.

The heat gun on the mat had a tidy coil mark under its nozzle. A faint sweetness hung around it, the ghost of warmed resin and ribbon sealant. Next to it sat a little pile of trimmed edges, narrow and precise. One, half hidden under a tape dispenser, stopped Tessa's eye. Blush silk with a painted ivy trail in soft green, wired edge, 38 millimetres wide. She had seen the same shade on the hall banner, a match for the bride's scheme. She did not pounce. She lifted a hand toward the tray of spools instead.

"Beautiful dye lots," she said.

"Greybridge Mills," Vera said. "They get edge tone right. Most mills serve pine green as a default. Greybridge understands ivy is grey in shadow and blue in shade. Clients do not know why the room feels calm. This is why."

Tessa filed the name and the width. She did not trap herself with exact numbers out loud. She looked past the tray to the heat gun. "You use that on edges."

"To relax ribbon where the wire fights you," Vera said. "To warm adhesive when a clamp would mar a surface. To ease tape for clean removal. Also for shrinking heat sleeves on cables when a DJ tries to turn a wedding into a hazard course." She lifted the gun, checked the cord with reflex care, and set it down again. "We do not point hot air at banisters."

"I will note your restraint," Mabel said.

Vera ignored the edge of that and set a small plastic tub on the bench. Inside sat a nest of test tiles. She pulled one free and showed a line of glue samples dried across a tile in neat bands, each strip numbered, each strip labeled with a stick-on dot. "We train on scrap," she said. "My staff can tell you which adhesive will hold and which remover will let go without harm. The amateurs in this valley call everything glue, as if a clasp and a weld were cousins. I will educate them until I retire."

"What do you teach for porcelain," Tessa asked, keeping her tone open.

"Minimal heat, no brute force," Vera said. "A fast set gel can hold a handle long enough for a photograph. A slow cure is kinder to the body but fails in time pressure. You know this or you would not have reset Isla's cup without cracking it. Half the people in my trade would have delivered it back to the bride with a charming lecture about embracing imperfection. I refuse to sell lectures."

"Do you teach them to notice a stain line," Tessa asked.

"Any joint with age shows tea in the pores," Vera said, brisk. "If the seam is bright, the work is new. If a planner tries to sell you patina at short notice, ask to see her bin. It will be full of wipes."

Mabel coughed into her hand to hide a sound that was almost a laugh. Vera's eyes slid to her, then to Tessa. "You have questions you are not asking," she said.

"I have a few," Tessa said. "I am minding Inspector Shaw's rules. I came to see how you work and to collect details I can tuck into my understanding. You make it hard not to admire precision."

Vera accepted the compliment as her due. She turned the caddy so the labels faced Tessa more squarely. The Citrus Remover No. 12 bottle wore a manufacturer's sticker with a small citrus slice icon, a hazard diamond, and a code embossed in faint grey. Tessa read it without reading it aloud. CB12-PEEL. She did not know if the code meant anything beyond neat branding. She knew she would remember it at three in the morning.

"Tell me about the wedding account," Mabel said, shameless in service of motive. "People say Delia took Fernvale from you."

Vera did not flinch. She was honest about some things because it saved time. "She pitched her way into the committee with mood boards and phrases that sounded like grants," she said. "She underbid me for three months, then negotiated a rate that made catering cry. She called it community spirited. I call it vanity. She spoke the Trust's language about heritage and harmony and cohesion. She also liked to be seen at ribbon cuttings. I supply tables. She supplied applause."

"You did not care for applause," Tessa said.

"I care for a hall that pays suppliers and does not treat hire companies as an endless sponsorship," Vera said. "I care for economies that add up. Delia's budgets required someone to carry cost. It was never Delia."

"She cost you the account," Mabel said.

"She cost me the account," Vera agreed, even. "I learned from it. I adjusted my pitch to other villages. I do not hide grudges under lace. I fold them into margins."

"Did you handle the ivy banner at Fernvale this morning," Tessa asked lightly. "I admired the drape on the landing."

"Of course," Vera said. "Len installs like a man with a broom, so I trimmed the edges and softened the curl. If you saw a nice fall at the rail, you saw my work." She gave the heat gun a little pat as if to say, we made that together. "I also corrected the florist's loop length. Ivy prints do not want to sag. They want to hold a line. I gave them a line."

"The ribbon colour read as blush with a true green," Tessa said, as if complimenting. "Greybridge again."

"Lot 7B," Vera said before stopping herself. "Not that it matters to you."

"It matters to my eye," Tessa said. She let her gaze drift to the tiny pile of trimmed ends. The top sliver matched the banner shade. Its cut edge looked clean in most places and slightly glazed in one, a telltale of heat kissing the finish. No harm to the ribbon. Just a signature.

"You have staff," Mabel said. "Do they carry this caddy or do you attend personally to everything with a plug."

"I assign a senior to every Fernvale hire," Vera said. "Today I attended myself for the first hour. Then I went to the van for a tablecloth and a call. Then I returned to the anteroom because someone had let a crate block the route. I do not babysit Len and I do not collate chairs for bridesmaids."

"Who has access to your kit on site," Tessa asked.

"Me and my senior," Vera said. "If a junior touches removers without permission, they carry chairs for a month. If anyone pockets a wipe for home, I bin them. We have rules. That is why my clients receive goods in better condition than they deserve."

"Where were you when the shout went up," Mabel asked.

"In the hall near the flowers," Vera said. "Looking at everyone with hands while praying for fewer hands." She paused, then added, clipped but not unfeeling, "I did not like Delia, but I did not wish her harm. I can hold both truths."

Tessa let that hang. She believed Vera's devotion to process and reputation, if not her capacity for mercy. She looked again at the caddy. The Citrus No. 12 bottle had a flip spout with a pin hole. The cap wore a micro smear of clear substance near the hinge, the kind a person leaves when they wipe a droplet with a cloth.

The scent above it was unmistakable now she was near. Sharp peel, cleaner than furniture oil, leaner than orange. The same family as the newel cap. She did not say so. She reached for a different question instead.

"Do you keep brand logs," she asked. "If you rotated to a new remover last month, I would love to know what you abandoned."

Vera tilted her head as if weighing whether to be generous. "I do keep logs," she said. "I trialled No. 10 last winter. It bloomed on high gloss under flash. No. 12 behaves. If a planner has a problem with a dull patch, I tell her to polish properly next time. I am not a janitor. I am a supplier."

"The difference is large," Mabel said, tart. "Shall we be plain. You own the good wipes. Len owns a bucket. Delia owned taste. Today the floor owned all three."

Vera's eyes sharpened. "Delia pushed for shine," she said. "She would have pushed a man into the canal if it suited her plan. I supplied ribbon and clean cloth and a rail no longer smeared by human oils. The rest lives with whoever polished."

Tessa let silence sit for a breath. Then she turned to the arch on the bench. Silk ivy wound up its side in a measured helix. The stem ties were invisible from a metre away. Close up, she saw how they had been fixed. A dot of gel, a quick press with a silicone finger, a puff of warm air to set the curl. Nothing sloppy. Nothing sentimental.

"You do good work," she said, as if she were only a colleague paying a colleague.

"Of course I do," Vera said. "If I did not, Delia would never have noticed me enough to take my account."

The line lay there. Vera did not pick it up. She was not careless with sentences.

A driver appeared at the bay door with a clipboard. "V," he said, "the Broadoak return has two chipped plates and a napkin with wax on it. Tell me whether you want me to invoice or sigh."

"Photograph, invoice, then sigh," Vera said. "Seal the box. No one lifts anything without a look. I am busy."

He vanished. The brief exchange left another smell to place. Candle wax, citrus, starch. Tessa's mind arranged the triangle and set the heat gun at one point. She looked back to the tiny pile of ribbon ends. The top offcut had a curl that matched the landing drape. The narrowest sliver along one side had a faint tack, as if it had brushed something that still had a voice. Not sticky. Only present.

"Your bench is a museum of near misses," Mabel murmured.

"Near misses are called experience," Vera said.

Tessa checked her watch, then smiled as if apologising. "We will leave you to your returns. Thank you for showing me the kit."

"I expect the courtesy to be repaid," Vera said. "If I need a china handle pulled back from the brink, I will call rather than watch a planner ruin a relic."

"My bench is open by appointment," Tessa said.

Vera slid an invoice across the steel with that neat hand. "For Len," she said. "He will insist on paying cash and filing a receipt under despair. Tell him I accept card."

Mabel took the paper and tucked it into her bag. She had a talent for making paperwork feel safe. "We will hand deliver," she said.

As they walked the aisle toward daylight, Tessa stopped once, casual as a person admiring crates. A hook by the exit held a key ring with a little tin teapot fob, a spare for the van. She looked and did not linger. Teapots were everywhere once you started counting them. It was like ivy on a fence. You saw the first leaf, then the pattern spread.

Outside the roller door, the canal lay green and slow. Dragonflies stitched light to water. Bramble drank from a travel bowl with the discipline of a small soldier. Mabel shaded her eyes and said nothing until they had crossed the service yard and turned onto the quiet lane.

"You have a face," she said finally.

"I have three pieces lining up," Tessa said. "Citrus No. 12 in a bottle with a peel bite. Heat gun used this morning on ribbon to set a drape. Ribbon ends on the bench in Isla's blush and ivy. Vera knows her adhesives. She lost the Fernvale account to Delia and she admits it without apology."

"And you smelled the same peel on the newel," Mabel said.

"I did," Tessa said. "Len's wax smells like bees and paraffin with a hint of kitchen lemon. It sits warm on wood. No. 12 sits sharp and leaves no hand. If you wipe a varnished cap with it, you do not leave shine, you take it."

"And if a person gripped there," Mabel said.

"Their palm would find less purchase," Tessa said. "On an over buffed landing, less purchase is one turn of the screw."

Mabel let the picture settle. "You will not deliver that sentence to Shaw like a gift."

"I will not," Tessa said. "I will bring him my nose and the label and the width of the ribbon. He prefers facts to frames."

"Good," Mabel said. "Frames can be pretty and wrong."

They walked the long way back to Ivy Lane because the long way let a mind pack its drawer without spilling anything. At the corner where the baker sets out a chalkboard, Tessa stopped and wrote three lines in her notebook with her back against the wall.

Vera kit: Citrus Remover No. 12, code CB12-PEEL, distinct peel scent. Heat gun on bench warm, ribbon offcuts blush with ivy, 38 mm, Greybridge Mills, Lot 7B. Vera admits trimming landing banner and wiping rail.

She added, small and private, do not accuse, do not assume. Then she closed the book.

At Ink & Ivy, the hatbox waited on the top shelf like an egg in a nest. The seam on the cup had settled to a quiet line. Tessa lifted the lid and looked as if checking a sleeping child. The handle behaved.

The bell chimed. The young constable poked his head in with a smile that managed to be human inside an afternoon that had not been kind. "Inspector Shaw says thank you," he said. "He also says if you happen to pass along any brand names for cleaners you mentioned, write them, not tell them, because phones forget detail."

"Phones forget what you think they will remember," Mabel said.

"People do as well," the constable said. "We rely on people anyway."

Tessa tore a square from her pad and wrote Citrus Remover No. 12, code CB12-PEEL. Heat gun present on bench at Locke & Linen. Ribbon offcut blush with ivy print, Greybridge Mills Lot 7B. She folded the note and gave it to him.

"Hand to Shaw only," she said.

"Understood," he said. "He likes his own pockets."

When the door had settled and the bell had stopped its soft echo, Mabel poured tea. Bramble sighed and set his chin on his paws. The day did not soften, but it sat down.

"You see it," Mabel said.

"I see enough to know where I must not jump," Tessa said. "Vera's kit could explain the cap without a crime. It could also explain a choice. People tidy, improve, correct, remove. They do it for photographs and pride. They do it for invoices. Sometimes they do it because they are angry at a woman who took their account."

"And sometimes," Mabel said, "they do it because their hand likes power."

Tessa drank, set the mug down, and stroked the notebook cover with one thumb. "Inspector Shaw will test the residue on the rail. He will place time around the saucer. He will count keys. We will keep our heads. We will not fill the quiet with story."

"We will wait for the next piece to present itself," Mabel said. "It always does. Stories are show-offs."

Bramble's ears tipped. A shadow passed the glass. When the bell chimed, it did so with a small bright sound that made Tessa look up with a steadier heart. The day had not finished wanting her attention. It rarely did.

FIVE

The Laurel Trust kept its offices on the first floor of an old malt house overlooking the canal. The brick had been scrubbed into respectability and the brass letters on the door were polished within an inch of vanity. Inside, the foyer smelled of old paper and new policy. A framed mission statement hung above a radiator, flanked by photographs of the hall in every season, each one captioned as if it had won a prize.

A receptionist with a neat fringe and a neat smile asked their names and whether they had an appointment. Mabel produced an appointment out of thin air by setting Vera's invoice on the counter and saying, with cheerful authority, "Procurement will want this signed before month end, dear."

"Of course," the receptionist said, as if people said such things to her all day. "Mr Hale is in. He asked to be disturbed only by common sense."

"We brought two servings," Mabel said.

Martin Hale's office had a view of the canal and a view of himself. Tidy shelves, tidy desk, tidy trophies of committee life. A framed brochure mock-up rested on the credenza, the kind with a white margin and tasteful ivy. The window was open a crack; the breeze lifted a page on a stack of drafts and let it fall again with a papery sigh.

Martin stood when they entered. He had a politician's handshake and a financier's watch. "Ms Harper," he said. "Mrs Clegg. Come in. Tea?"

"Only if it does not require a committee," Mabel said, sitting. "We brought paperwork."

Tessa stayed standing a moment longer to take in the desk without being rude about it. A laptop sat open to a page with a green header and a crest of laurel leaves. She did not squint. She did not need to. She had seen the same design on the notice board in the hall. The line at the top read A Shared Heritage, A Living Hall. On the desk pad, under a paperweight shaped like a river stone, lay a draft memo with the heading Canal Gate, Phase One. She kept those words in her pocket along with the ribbon width and the bottle code.

Martin took the invoice from Mabel, glanced at the total, and made an approving noise. "At last, something that can be ticked," he said. "Len will thank you. He pretends not to care about order, then sulks when the world fails to supply it."

"Len would like the world to stop polishing itself under his feet," Mabel said.

"Wouldn't we all," Martin replied, not entirely unkind. He looked at Tessa. "How can I help you without making more work for us both."

"We came to drop that," Tessa said, nodding at the invoice,

"and to ask a housekeeping question before it becomes a future scuffle. Donation crates."

Martin folded his hands. The gesture said he was pleased to have moved from grief to something he could manage. "Yes. Mr Porter has a generous eye for what belongs to the Barn," he said. "We have a process on paper. It is not yet a process in practice. I intend to correct that."

"Before or after a vintage saucer goes out on a Saturday morning," Tessa asked, mild.

His gaze sharpened a degree. "You have heard about the saucer."

"Everyone has heard," Mabel said. "Gwen at the Barn could pipe the traffic report if she wished."

"I would not expect the Barn to distinguish between the council's plain china and a family piece," he said. "That is not a judgement, it is a reality. The hall has a jumble habit. We must cure it."

"You hold the key cure," Tessa said, and gestured toward the ledger on a side table. "Sign in, sign out, no exceptions, and a second pair of eyes when the crate is packed."

Martin nodded, pleased to be told something he already thought. "Quite. And volunteers who understand that a storeroom is not the village attic. Hence the draft," he said, and lifted the paperweight so he could tap the memo headed Canal Gate, Phase One. "We will tidy both access and exit. If the gate is to become our second entrance for larger events, we must present a grown-up face. Lists. Lighting. People in the right place. You know how this works. A room looks effortless when the work is hidden."

Tessa looked at the heading again and did not look at all. Canal Gate, Phase One. On the credenza, the brochure board showed a paragraph with a green line under it. The words were large enough to be legible at a distance. She read them because the room had invited her to. The Laurel Trust will deliver cohesion through a clear route plan, stewarded access at Canal Gate, and a single source of truth for booking and procurement. A single source of truth. The phrase had the smoothness of a pressed leaf. On the memo under the paperweight, a bullet point read, in smaller type, Deliver cohesion through a clear route plan, stewarded access at Canal Gate, and single-source procurement. Recycled, not quoted. She filed it with care.

"Procurement," Mabel said, as if tasting a lemon. "You do love that word."

"It keeps me from saying spending," Martin said. "Procurement is the adult cousin. It suggests control."

"You are also fond of cohesion," Tessa said.

"It plays well in board papers," he said, honest and unbothered. "People like the sense that their hall fits like a glove into a story about the town. The council likes phrases that make spreadsheets look like bridges. We write for the audience we have."

"And the audience today," Mabel said, "is a village that watched a woman fall."

Martin's face changed a shade. Not a flinch. A tightening of something under the skin. "Delia knew how to ask for shine," he said, measured. "She pushed. She also handled risk with a decorator's belief that if you cannot see it, it does not exist. I would prefer we do not litigate the dead in my office."

"No one is litigating," Tessa said. "We are placing facts in their boxes. Some of those boxes live in your drawers."

He passed a hand over his hair, a tidy circuit. "Ms Harper, are you here as a citizen or as a consultant. If the latter, I must ask for an hourly rate."

"As a citizen," Tessa said. "Paid in tea."

"That I can afford," he said, and reached to the intercom. "Sian, would you mind."

While they waited, Tessa let her gaze return to the laptop screen. The page showed the Trust's web brochure in desktop view. A section titled Why Fernvale Hall Matters carried three short paragraphs nested under a header that matched the framed poster in the foyer. The second paragraph began with a phrase that prickled because she had just read it twice. Stewarded access, single-source booking, cohesive events calendar. On the desk, the memo under the paperweight used the same string with a comma out of place. It was not an accident of similar minds. It was a cut and paste wearing a new shirt.

Sian arrived with a tray that reconciled milk, sugar, and municipal biscuits. She put it down with a deftness learned in rooms where cups make allies. Martin poured as if he had spent a life doing it between votes.

"Back to your question," he said. "We will add a double check to the morning procedure. Mr Porter will not dispatch anything without a second signature. Keys will be signed out to people with names, not to committees with moods. Spare B has been a nuisance since Christmas."

"Spare B is also missing," Tessa said. "Your ledger shows it signed out in Vera Locke's tidy hand at nine fifteen for the anteroom. Returned before noon, perhaps without its little hat."

"Vera's hands are tidy because she understands payment," Martin said. "I do not love her invoices. I prefer her methods to ad hoc arrangements."

"And yet," Mabel said, "Delia walked your budget into applause anyway."

"She did," he said simply. "We fought about it. She won while she breathed." He set his cup down. His ring made a small sound against the china. "You have a look that says you have come to ask for something you should not have yet."

"I would like a copy of your key policy draft," Tessa said. "I would also like a copy of anything that touches Canal Gate. It is easier to be a helpful citizen when one knows where the bollards will be."

He considered, then decided generosity cost less than withholding. He slid the memo out from under the paperweight, made a duplicate at the printer, and handed her the copy. "Read, then pretend it arrived by magic," he said. "In return, you will encourage your friends to volunteer for steward shifts in October. People love a gala until they are asked to wear a high-vis vest."

"I look dreadful in yellow," Mabel said. "But I wield a clipboard like a sword."

"That will do," he said.

Tessa glanced down not for content, which she would absorb later, but for confirmation. The memo carried the heading she had seen, the trio of phrases she had read on the web page and the poster, and a bullet list of tasks that included Key registry to be audited by end of month and Spare hooks to be relabelled with neutral rings. At the bottom, under Actions, someone had typed Draft vendor list for single-source pilot. She did not entirely approve of pilots that ate markets, but she kept that for later too.

"You intend to keep events at Fernvale by bundling work into packages that travel less," she said, conversational rather than combative. "Single invoices, single contacts, less drift to hotels and barns. You will call it cohesion."

"I will call it efficiency," he said. "We lose bookings to out-of-town venues when brides tire of coordinating between five suppliers. If we can offer a smooth path through Canal Gate to a hall dressed and ready, we keep the spend here. That money supports the choir, the Scouts, the roof. We have to make the case in language that lands."

"And if suppliers outside your list find themselves frozen out," Mabel said, "you will call that regrettable."

"I will call it competition," he said. "Ms Locke knows how to compete. She did not lose Fernvale because of my list. She lost it because Delia wanted control and a discount. That, and a certain appetite for being photographed with ribbon."

He said photographed with the exact curved contempt Tessa had expected. It was not the contempt that interested her; it was the sentence that came next.

"We cannot run a hall on mood," he said. "We run it on schedules, packages, and language that makes grant panels nod. If you think that cynical, think of your heating bill."

"I think of Canal Gate," Tessa said. "Phase One suggests there is a Phase Two."

He smiled. "There is always a Phase Two," he said. "Lighting, resurfacing, improved access for suppliers. We start with stewarding and signage. We end with a revenue line that means we do not hold out a bucket every spring. In my old firm we called that survival."

"Your old firm wrote brochures," Mabel said.

"My old firm wrote anything people needed to hear," he said. "Which is not the indictment you think it is. Words pay for roofs when the roofers want cash."

He lifted another sheet from the stack and frowned at a paragraph. The title read Autumn Gala Sponsorship Pack. Midway down the page, a sentence leaped up with a flourish because it had leaped up on the brochure and the web page too. A hall to trust, a place to gather. He crossed out a comma and put it back without the comma. The rhythm matched the poster in the foyer. Habit, not thought. Tessa watched the act and watched herself not smile.

Outside the window a barge moved under the bridge with the slow majesty of anything that ignores schedules. Martin watched it too, then set the paper down as if he had given himself permission to soften for a breath. "How is Isla," he asked, almost quiet.

"She is upright," Mabel said. "Her family is doing the good work. People have stopped asking her to sit down quite as often."

"Good," he said. "Delia would have hated a garden ceremony. She would have called the light uncooperative. I prefer it already."

The receptionist knocked and stepped in with a blue folder. "The council sent the updated wording for the heritage grant," she said. "They marked up the bit about single-source."

Martin took the folder, scanned the page, then smiled without humor. "They speak my language back to me," he said. "Useful and faintly alarming."

"They lifted your phrase," Tessa said lightly. "A hall to trust."

"They lifted all of it," he said. "I will sue for royalties." He looked up. "You see why I write carefully. Words travel. If I am not mindful, they return wearing someone else's shoes."

"And sometimes," Tessa said, "they walk from your web page onto your memos without changing shoes at all."

He met her eyes. He was not a fool. "We like to keep the story consistent," he said. "The council calls that alignment. I call it muscle memory. If you are accusing me of thinking in headings, I plead guilty."

"Not accusing," Tessa said. "Noting. It helps me predict where you will put bollards and banners. If I want to avoid tripping, I need to hear your music."

He relaxed a fraction. "Then hear this. We will keep events at Fernvale. We must. Every time a wedding goes to a hotel in the next town, we lose a week of life. Len loses hours, the choir loses a rehearsal slot, the hall loses the excuse to be useful. If I press, it is because the hall cannot speak for itself. It has me."

"And your phrases," Mabel said.

"And my phrases," he agreed.

He signed Vera's invoice with a pen that looked like it had its own pension. He slid it back to Mabel and rose to signal the end of pleasantness.

On the way out, the foyer poster caught Tessa's eye again. A Shared Heritage, A Living Hall. The second line of small print was the same sentence she had watched him cross-check on his memo. She did not need a magnifying glass to hear the echo. She imagined his hand on both. She imagined how often he had read those words to himself until they stopped meaning anything except budget.

They took the stairs down to the street because the lift always smelled like recent plans. On the landing, a cork board held volunteer sign-up sheets. One read Canal Gate Steward Rota, Autumn Gala. Another read Donation Crew, Saturday Mornings. Two lines down someone had added, in small tidy letters, No boxes leave without two signatures. Mabel tapped the note with her fingertip.

"He does listen," she said.

"He listens when it suits," Tessa said. "Which is not a sin, only a trait."

They walked out into a day that had not made up its mind about rain. The canal wore a lid of pale cloud. A moorhen scissored past as if late for a meeting. Bramble paused to watch it with professional interest and then trotted on.

At the corner, Tessa stopped under a plane tree and opened the memo copy. She read the heading again. Canal Gate, Phase One. The bullet points were practical and dull in a way that made them dangerous when ignored. Stewarded access, single-source booking, cohesive calendar. The same string appeared in the paragraph at the top with a rhythm she could hum now. She wrote, on her own pad beside it, memo language matches web brochure and foyer poster; likely written by Martin in both places; phrase set used to sell procurement, now used to steer it.

Mabel peered. "You plan to tell Shaw that our uncle writes his own chorus."

"I plan to tell him that if he is looking for where influence sits, it is here," Tessa said, tapping the heading. "This is not murder. It is motive's cousin. If a person wanted Delia out of the way because she would not play the single-source game, this language would be the hymnbook. If a person wanted a certain supplier in, same book."

"Do you think Martin wanted Delia out of the way," Mabel asked.

"I think Martin wanted control and predictability," Tessa said.

"Delia did not give him either. Control buys roofs. It also buys enemies. Whether an enemy uses a floor is another question."

"And whether a floor used an enemy," Mabel said.

Tessa folded the memo, slid it into her bag, and wrote a neat line in her notebook.

Trust memo recycles brochure phrasing; Canal Gate, Phase One; single-source pilot listed; language lifted from web. Pressure to keep events at hall; package procurement. Watch for who benefits.

She added another, smaller.

Note: foyer poster shares the exact sentence; Martin edits comma to match.

On Ivy Lane, the bell at Ink & Ivy chimed as if to say time for work, not politics. Tessa put the kettle on because routine has power, then climbed the little ladder to check the hatbox on the high shelf. The handle had settled into its place like a thought that finally fits. She felt the quick quiet of a job that held.

The bell chimed again. Detective Inspector Shaw stepped in as if he had always had a key to the village and only borrowed it today. He looked less like a storm and more like a barometer at steady. He glanced toward the hatbox, toward Bramble, toward Tessa's face.

"You have been to see Mr Hale," he said. "How many phrases did he use before tea."

"Enough to buy a roof," Tessa said. "I brought you a copy of his memo, and a note about his headings. The web page sings the same song."

"Good," he said. "My constable is checking the Barn's log against the van's tracker. If the saucer went in before the fall, it tells us something about timing. If a wipe lifted varnish at the rail, the lab will hum it back to me by morning. Words are helpful. Residue sings louder."

He did not sit. He did not rush. He took the memo with two

fingers, as if paper could bruise, and tucked it into a folder without reading it.

"Anything else I should know before I ask the wrong person at the wrong moment," he asked.

"Keys," Tessa said. "Spare B wore a teapot and went walking. Vera wrote her name in the book after someone left a line blank. Martin had Canal Gate yesterday and the day before, and he is building a list that would keep the hall's money inside these walls."

"Everyone likes a list when they hold the pen," Shaw said. "Thank you. Do not get run over by a committee."

"I never cross in front of one," Tessa said.

When he had gone, Mabel reached for the biscuit tin, selected the least hopeful custard cream, and split it with a practised twist.

"Your face again," she said. "What is it now."

"Only this," Tessa said, and smiled despite herself. "If a phrase appears on a poster, a web page, and a memo, someone is either very tidy or very determined. Either way, you can follow it like a ribbon. It will take you to a hand."

"Let us see whose hand it is willing to take," Mabel said.

Bramble thumped his tail twice, the exact number of a small agreement. The kettle clicked. Outside, a barge horn sounded once, polite as a knock. The village breathed. Tessa reached for her cup and, for a moment, allowed the ordinary to settle over everything that was not.

SIX

Saturday afternoons at Ink & Ivy carried a rhythm all their own. Repairs lined up like polite supplicants on the bench. Glue caps sat in a row, labels facing forward as if they hoped for promotion. The bell chimed in pairs rather than singles, couples collecting frames, grandparents with boxes of old cards, children who brought broken pencils as if a fresh point could mend a week.

Tessa cleared a square of space, wiped the mat, and checked the hatbox high on the shelf. The handle on Isla's cup had settled. The seam held its quiet line, no bloom, no shift. She nodded to it the way a person nods to a kettle that has behaved. Bramble lay under the bench with his chin on his paws and an opinion about biscuits."

Mabel arrived with a canvas tote that looked as if it had served at every fete since 1989. She dropped it on the counter with a flourish that promised entertainment. "I bring treasure," she announced, "and trouble disguised as ribbon."

"If the treasure is in fact ribbon, I will need tea," Tessa said.

"Tea is implied," Mabel said, and pulled out two spools and a tangle of ends. "The Barn had a basket near the door marked Odd Lengths. I promised Ruth I would turn them into bunting for the library. I also promised not to set fire to anything, which shows a lack of faith."

Tessa tilted the first spool. The cardboard core had softened with age until it felt like a soft roll between her fingertips. The second spool carried a faded mill label beneath a run of thread. Greybridge Mills, handwritten price, someone's hurried 70p in pencil. The ribbon itself was a tame cream. Nothing like the blush ivy from the hall. She filed the mill in her head anyway, a familiar name in a village that reused everything.

"Cut me strips," Mabel said. "Your hand is straight."

"My hand is obedient," Tessa said. She lifted the scissors and found a beat in her head that kept lengths even. Bramble shifted, then sat up with a flick of attention. He had the air of a clerk sensing a ledger.

"Not for you," Mabel told him. "Unless you have developed a taste for satin."

Bramble ignored the warning and came to inspect the tote. He pushed his nose into the canvas as if he had been assigned to customs. Something in the smell interested him. He snuffled at the cream spool, then at the faded one. He tapped the older spool with his paw, then nudged the cardboard core with his nose until it rolled. A small sound came from inside, a faint metallic tick against paper.

"What have you there," Tessa asked.

Bramble nosed the core again with precision. A tiny brass

rectangle slid from the inner seam and skittered across the mat with a bright ping. It came to rest against the scissors, caught by a smear of resin on the blade that held it like a pause.

Mabel leaned in. "That did not come with bunting."

"No," Tessa said. "It came with purpose."

She lifted the brass between thumb and forefinger. It was the size of a fingernail, a little thicker, edges filed smooth. A small hole at one end would take a split ring or a wire. On one face, stamped clean and proud, sat a laurel leaf. Not a sprig, not a wreath, only a single leaf with midrib and vein. The stamp had depth. A tool had bitten it, not a decorator's press.

"Trust leaf," Mabel murmured.

"Their crest uses a pair," Tessa said. "This is one."

She turned it. The reverse showed faint adhesive shadow at one edge, a clear strip no wider than a match. Not fresh. Not ancient either. Someone had stuck it to something that was not quite clean. The line had a small curl, as if peeled back once and stuck again.

"Where did you pick this basket," Tessa asked. "Front desk or back room."

"Front," Mabel said. "Gwen moved the odd lengths to the bell table after the morning rush. She likes to sell ribbon to people who want to tie hope around jars. I bought the lot because the library refuses to teach knots."

"Did you see who priced it," Tessa asked.

"Dot, I think," Mabel said. "She was sticking fifty pence on anything that did not scream furniture."

Tessa glanced at the inside of the core. A strip of old paper lined it where the cardboard had split and been reinforced. The lining paper had not quite met the edge in one place. Behind it, down in the tunnel of the spool, she saw a paler corner. She tilted the spool and the corner shifted. Not part of the core. A folded scrap tucked into the hollow, flattened by years.

"Tweezers," she said, and fetched a pair from the drawer.

She eased the scrap out slowly so it would not tear further. It came, inch by inch, like a secret that wanted to be handled, then lay in her palm, cross-grain to itself from long pressure. She unfolded it once. The paper had lines faint as threads and numbers in two columns. Dates down the left, sums in pounds and pence on the right. No headings, no names. Along the top edge the tear had gone through a printed title. She could still read the end of one word and the whole of another.

…Gate Phase 1

She felt the little click in her head that comes when pieces sit next to one another and recognise kin. Canal Gate on a memo in Martin's office. Phase One on the heading. Here, on a torn stub, Phase 1. No Canal on the scrap, only Gate cut in half and gone. Enough to call it family.

"What is it," Mabel asked, peering as if reading tea leaves.

"A ledger fragment," Tessa said. "Someone kept totals. Someone tore this page out across the title."

She held it under the light. The type was not from a home printer. The ink sat sharp, no feather. A faint grid ghosted through from the missing page beneath, the kind used on accounting pads sold to people who like straight columns. The paper carried the chalk-dry feel of stock ordered by a committee. Near the lower edge, faint smudges read as fingers in a hurry.

She looked back at the brass tab. The laurel leaf stamp was deeper than a costume trinket. A small notch marred the lower edge, as if it had been flicked off a press frame or snapped cleanly from a strip. If you wanted to rivet small tabs to boards or boxes, you would make a row and snap them free as needed.

"Where did this spool live before the Barn," Tessa asked. "Do you know."

"Ruth said the ribbon came from a hall clear-out last autumn," Mabel said. "She said Vera brought a crate of offcuts and workable remnants after the Harvest Fair. People buy ribbon to soothe themselves. We sold scores. This one may have sat in the back until a week ago. The basket had a sign in Dot's handwriting that said Good for bows."

"Good as hiding place too," Tessa said.

Bramble watched her with the solemnity of a small clerk who has found a coin in the till and expects praise. Tessa gave him a biscuit because even in a case without a case, rewards matter. He ate it without crumbs because he had standards.

Tessa set both finds on a clean tray, then fetched two glassine envelopes from the cupboard where she kept archival sleeves. She wrote labels in a neat hand. Brass tab, laurel stamp, recovered from ribbon spool at 14:32. Ledger stub, torn, "Phase 1" visible, recovered from same spool. Chain of custody mattered less for citizens than for officers; she kept it anyway. Her bench habits had taught her to treat paper kindly and time precisely.

Mabel perched on the stool with one heel hooked like a schoolgirl. "You will ring Shaw."

"I will," Tessa said. "He asked me to give him paper, not stories."

"He is learning," Mabel said.

Before Tessa reached the phone, the bell chimed and the young constable put his head around the door with his hat in his hand and the kind of careful step people use when they fear glass. "Ms Harper," he said, apologetic. "Inspector Shaw asked me to check whether you found anything that smells like an afternoon with paperwork."

"Two things," Tessa said. "Your timing is theatrical."

He came to the bench. Tessa laid out the tray like a breadboard. The constable leaned without looming, eyes narrowing in the way of people who take pride in seeing. "That is a laurel," he said. "And that looks like a piece from a book I would not be allowed to borrow."

"Ledger," Tessa said. "The title is torn. The phrase appears again. Phase 1. It repeats in Martin's draft and on the Trust web page."

He did not touch. "Where."

"In the core of a ribbon spool from the Barn," she said. "Bramble fished the tab out by force of nose. The paper sat behind a lining strip."

The constable's mouth quirked. "I will add him to the payroll."

"He takes payment in biscuits and praise," Mabel said.

"I am rich in both," he said.

Tessa passed him the glassine envelopes. He looked at the labels and nodded, then slid the tray closer to photograph the items with his phone. He measured the tab against a steel rule from the pen cup and read the length aloud for the recording. He took a wide shot of the spool, the core, the lining strip, and the loose ribbon. He opened his notebook and wrote the time, the room, the people, the dog.

"Inspector will be here in ten," he said. "I will step outside and tell him we have a leaf and a list."

"Leaf and list," Mabel said. "It sounds like a pub."

"Fernvale needs a new pub name," Tessa said. "The Dog and Battery has outlived its joke."

The constable laughed, then remembered his position and smoothed his face. "Back in a moment."

When he had gone, Tessa lifted the mill label on the faded spool and slid a fingernail under the edge. No hidden notes there. Only old gum and the faintest scent of the cupboard where someone had kept it away from light. She ran the ribbon once between two fingers. The weave held, no snag. Whoever had tucked the stub inside had cared enough to leave the ribbon untouched. Either neatness or haste. People who hide things leave marks that feel like personality.

"Who hides a tab and a ledger piece in a donation basket," Mabel asked. "Someone who wants the tab back later without carrying it through a front door."

"Someone who wants to move a thing through a room quietly,"

Tessa said. "The Barn is a good throat. Things go in, then out, and no one remembers the middle."

"Gwen will remember now," Mabel said. "She will hunt anyone who thinks of her back room as a courier."

The bell chimed again. Inspector Shaw stepped in with his folder and his steady weather. He took in the bench, the tray, the dog, the ribbon, then looked at Tessa with the lift of a person who has learnt not to be surprised when the same shop produces both glue and clues.

"Leaf," he said.

"Leaf," Tessa said, and handed him the glassine.

He turned the tab over in the sleeve under the light. "Trust motif," he said. "I will confirm."

"Stamped deep," Tessa said. "Not a costume charm."

He held the stub to the light and read the numbers. Three figures, two figures, pence columns full of zeros or odd pennies. Someone had totalled in a neat office hand. The tear had run through the title along the top. The words left behind made a shape in the air even if the letters had gone.

"Phase 1," he read. "And Gate cut in half."

"Your memo," Tessa said, not as a challenge. "Martin's heading repeats here. The web page repeats the same three words."

"Words repeat in towns with plans," Shaw said. "Plans repeat phrases until they feel like law."

He photographed both items, then signed the labels below Tessa's name and added his own time. He glanced at Mabel. "You brought the ribbon."

"I bought it," she said. "Do not charge me with theft when I have the receipt for fifty pence and a lecture about storage."

"Where," he asked.

"The front table, left of the till," she said. "Odd Lengths. Ruth priced. Gwen stacked."

He nodded. "We will look. Do you know who donated the

basket."

"Ruth thought it came in with the hall crate last autumn," Mabel said. "Vera brought offcuts. She is efficient with leftovers."

Shaw's expression did not twitch. "We will confirm," he said.

He laid the tab and the stub back on the tray and stood there with his pencil balanced in the usual way across his fingers. "Thank you," he said. "If you find more spools with opinions, ring me first and resist the urge to solve. Leave the ribbon to bunting unless the bunting talks."

"Understood," Tessa said.

"Anything else," he asked, which he often did when he suspected the room had withheld a sentence out of courtesy.

"Only this," Tessa said. "The tab hole would take a split ring. The adhesive shadow suggests it sat on something smooth before someone stuck it to something else. If your evidence box of donor plaques includes small tags, this might match the set."

"And the stub," he said.

"The paper stock matches the Trust tone," Tessa said. "Committee paper. It feels like every agenda I have ever held to stop it blowing away in a car park. The font on the title looks like the brochure."

He acknowledged both without a promise. "I will not conjure provenance from adjectives," he said. "I will ask a printer."

"You will ask two," Mabel said. "Printers enjoy being right."

Shaw smiled, a small one. "I will ask three."

He lifted the tray and set it into a rigid folder that had foam inserts cut for objects. He had the air of a person moving eggs through a crowded room. When he had secured everything, he looked at Bramble.

"Promotion," he said.

"Biscuits and praise," Mabel said.

"I can afford both," Shaw said.

He left with the constable, who held the door and treated the bell as evidence too. The shop settled back around the space they vacated. Outside, someone laughed near the bakery and then remembered, and the sound fell away to something kind.

Tessa turned back to the bench. She took the faded spool, lifted the loose lining strip, and looked along the inside again in case the tunnel held another scrap. Empty. She put the spool aside for bunting and pulled the canvas tote closer. At the bottom lay a little tangle of offcuts that looked like a knot of snakes. She shook them out with care. One piece caught the light and showed a faint ivy print in a tired grey. Old stock. Not Greybridge's Lot 7B blush. Nothing to tie to a morning's drape. She let the tension in her shoulders slide an inch.

Mabel slid onto the customer stool with the relief of someone who has done their good deed and would now like jam. "We have a leaf that points to the Trust and a stub that hums Martin's song," she said. "If we were unkind we would knock on his door with both and enjoy his face."

"We will be kind," Tessa said. "We will let the officer with the pencil knock."

"You disappoint me," Mabel said with sweetness. "I thought you were born for theatre."

"I prefer rehearsal in my head," Tessa said. "On stage, I prefer props."

She made a note on her pad because notes stopped days from sliding into each other.

Bramble's find: brass tab with laurel stamp from ribbon spool purchased at Barn 14:10. Ledger stub inside core, "Phase 1" visible, numbers in pounds and pence. Spool had Greybridge Mills label, old price. Offcuts mixed, nothing blush ivy.

She drew the leaf quickly, vein and midrib, and shaded where the stamp had bitten deepest. She drew the little hole and the rough where the tab had snapped free. She drew the torn edge of the stub with the title broken so that Gate hung without its first half. She marked the times. She looked at her drawing the way a person checks a door.

"Will you go to the library with me," Mabel asked. "I intend to charm a child into cutting triangles and reward them with a biscuit."

"In a moment," Tessa said. "I want to check the basket of odd lengths once more before Shaw's officers make it look like a nature documentary."

Mabel grinned. "They will be neat."

"They will," Tessa said. "Neat and suspicious."

They put the spools back into the tote, kept the faded one aside for cutting, then walked down Ivy Lane toward the Barn. The afternoon had slipped toward that hour when light does generous things to brick. The Barn door stood open. Gwen sorted a box of spoons and Ruth rearranged lamps with the authority of a woman who knew which shelf liked which shape.

"Back again," Ruth said, pleased. "If you want more ribbon, buy quickly. A woman from Broadoak bought ten yards for a wreath, and I am fresh out of opinions."

"We brought praise," Mabel said, "and a note from Inspector Shaw that you will accept without sighing."

Ruth did not sigh. She had seen worse. Tessa went to the bell table where odd lengths still nested in a basket. She lifted each roll without hope of glamour. No hollow held a second secret. The basket had only ribbon, twine, a skein of string that had known honest hands, and a lone golden bow that had lost its adhesive and its pride.

Gwen eyed the basket as if it had offended her. "I will stick a sign that says no couriers," she said. "People think my back room is a hole in a fence."

"Your back room is immaculate," Mabel said. "They will not like it if they bounce off order."

"I will make them bounce," Gwen said, and meant it.

Back at Ink & Ivy, the kettle had decided to be helpful. Tessa poured and let the mug warm her hands. She set the brass sketch under the glass on the counter beside the tiny pile of notes that had grown all week. She slid the word leaf under the word laurel and the words Phase 1 under the words Canal Gate. The arrangement looked like a page that had meant to be read together and been torn in half by someone with a habit of tidy violence.

Mabel bit into a biscuit and broke it neatly in two, one half for Tessa and one for Bramble. Bramble took his with care, then returned to the spot under the shelf where he liked to sit when he had done a good day's work. He rested his chin on his paws and looked at the hatbox and then at Tessa as if to say he would guard both.

"Tomorrow," Mabel said. "What will tomorrow bring."

"Keys," Tessa said. "Lists. Wires that turn into lines. A person who does not like how a sentence sounds the second time they hear it."

Mabel nodded. "And tea."

"Always tea," Tessa said.

She wrote one more line on her pad because it felt right to leave the day with a sentence that held still.

Leaf in brass points to Laurel; stub sings Phase 1; Barn sits in the middle like a ferry.

She closed the pad. The bell chimed for a pair collecting a mended frame. The day went on with the dignity of places that decide to keep going. Outside, the canal kept its slow breath. Inside, the dog slept and the cup held.

SEVEN

Saturday wore itself thin by late afternoon. Ink & Ivy held the kind of quiet that lets a mind stack its thoughts. Tessa moved the two glassine envelopes to a higher shelf, then checked Isla's cup once more. The reset seam sat calm, a pale line that did not ask for attention. Bramble lay with his nose on his paws, one eye cracked to keep an eye on biscuits. Mabel had gone to coax small triangles from schoolchildren for bunting and had promised to return with jam.

The bell sounded. Poppy Hartley came in as if the floor might judge her gait. She had her tote and a stiff jaw. A dusting of icing sugar had found the cuff of her cardigan, a tell the tidy miss when the day has bitten them. She looked at the ceiling, the hatbox, the dog, anywhere but Tessa's eyes.

"I need the cup," she said at once. "Or to see it. Or to have something to hold that is not my own temper."

"You can hold tea," Tessa said. "It behaves."

Poppy let herself be steered to the chair by the counter while the kettle did the simple work that people forget to praise. She sat on her right hand for a beat, then freed it and rubbed the heel of the other eye with her left. The motion gave Tessa the fact she had already filed twice this week: Poppy's watch sat on the left wrist, face inward, band scuffed exactly where a right hand would fasten it. When Poppy reached for the mug a minute later she took it in her right hand without thinking, stirred with her right, and put the spoon down with a tap that sounded like relief disguised as annoyance.

"I am sorry about this morning," she said, not an apology so much as a sentence that wanted to leave the room. "I said things I should not have said. To Len. To my mother. To a woman who cried in the ladies and then thanked me for a tissue as if that made us friends."

"You had a morning that would boil anyone," Tessa said.

Poppy cupped the mug as if warming her palms. She blew across the top, sipped, then exhaled. "Did you ever want something so much it felt like a bruise," she asked, and then flinched as if the word had been the wrong one. "Not the wedding. That is Isla's. Something that felt like a step you could take if one person would stop standing in your door."

"Yes," Tessa said. "It comes with a village. Doors look like suggestions until a person plants both hands and leans."

Poppy laughed once, without pleasure. "Delia leaned," she said. "She leaned on everything. I asked her for a letter last month, a simple statement about my bakes, a reference for a micro-loan. Small money, just to buy a better oven and a mixer that does not cry after ten minutes. She said no. She said she had to keep lines clean. She said if she wrote for me she would be writing for every person who thought they could ice a cupcake and call it a business. She did not even taste anything. She said she did not eat sugar."

"She liked control more than cakes," Tessa said.

"I know," Poppy said. "I knew what she was like. I thought she might bend for me because I am not a stranger, I am a person who moves chairs and knows when ribbon wants to be trimmed. She did not bend."

"Did you tell her what the letter would do," Tessa asked.

"I told her the bank wanted proof that I delivered for an events planner," Poppy said, voice tight. "That I could meet orders and keep schedules. I told her I would bake for free for two christenings and one funeral. She said she did not accept barter. She said I was a conflict of interest. She made conflict sound like a disease."

"You had words," Tessa said.

"We had words," Poppy said. "Last night at rehearsal we had words in the cloakroom when she told me not to fuss about the aisle length because it was her aisle and she knew its mind." Her mouth twisted. "She said, very sweet, that not everyone who bakes needs a loan, some of us need a hobby."

"Who heard," Tessa asked.

"Vera passed by," Poppy said. "Of course. She stood outside like a person who waits for a kettle then says she never wanted tea. Len heard part of it and pretended to hum. Uncle Martin was on his phone and pretended to be deaf. Isla did not hear. My mother heard later and told me to take my temper outside and fold napkins until it went soft."

"Good mother," Tessa said.

"I slammed a door," Poppy admitted. "Not on anyone. On air. It felt stupid the second it banged."

Tessa let that sit. Red on the page did not run if you did not pour water on it. She topped up Poppy's tea and pushed the biscuit plate closer. Poppy took one with her right hand, snapped it in two with her right thumb, and began to eat in clean halves, right to left.

"About the cup," Poppy said, returning to the thing that was safe. "Is it right now."

"It is right," Tessa said. "The handle sits where a hand expects it. Slow cure, good angle. No tea near it today."

Poppy's shoulders dropped a fraction. "Thank you," she whispered, then caught herself and cleared her throat. "That handle this morning. When Isla showed me, I wanted to throw the hatbox out of the nearest window. How do you even glue a handle on the wrong side."

"You do it quickly," Tessa said. "You do it for the camera, not for the hand."

Poppy scowled into her cup. "It was left, was it not. Set for a left grip."

"It was," Tessa said. "Left lean, slight proud. A right hand picking it up would feel the angle fight them."

"I am right handed," Poppy said at once, then frowned. "You know that. You have seen me scribble lists. Of course you know. I am right handed and I would never set a handle to fight my own cup."

"It is a useful fact to have on paper," Tessa said. "Facts save people from opinions."

"Put it on any paper you like," Poppy said. "Write it on my forehead. And if anyone tells you I would glue a thing crooked, I will march them to my kitchen and make them watch me pipe a hundred shells in under a minute. Even angry, my hands are straight."

"I believe you," Tessa said.

Poppy stared at the hatbox on the shelf as if it could offer public absolution. "I hated Delia for saying no," she said without embellishment. "I did not hate her enough to push her down a stair. I am not built like that."

"No one is built like that until they find they are," Tessa said, gentle. "The job is to see who found it in themselves. The job is not yours."

Poppy nodded, then swallowed and lifted her chin. "You saw the saucer news."

"I heard the time," Tessa said. "The Barn logged the crate before the fall."

"Which means," Poppy said slowly, running the thought out to the end, "whoever removed it did that while we were still arranging flowers and arguing over chair angles."

"Or moving crate routes," Tessa said. "Len had the charity pickup early. The crate moved through that lobby like a small ship."

Poppy bared her teeth in a smile that had nothing to do with joy. "Vera told Len to move the sign," she said. "She talks to men like that, all ironed and bright. I wanted to tip lemon oil into her shoes."

Tessa noted the lemon without noting it. "What did you do after you slammed the door," she asked, steering her back to last night.

"I went outside," Poppy said. "I walked the cigarette strip though I do not smoke. I came back in when Isla needed me for bows. Then we did the run once, flowers and chairs, and Delia told the photographer where to stand even though it was rehearsal. I went home and rolled tart shells and pretended pastry is better therapy than honesty."

"And this morning," Tessa said. "Start to siren."

"I got to the hall at eight," Poppy said, right hand counting on the counter without being asked. "I had the crate with the teacups, the family ones, and a box with spare napkins. I let myself in with the key from Len. I put the saucers on the table, circle out, checked the hairline on the heirloom one was at the back where it would not read. I made two lists and stuck one under the salt. Delia came in at half past with ribbon and glare. Vera arrived near nine with a roll of tone and a comment about the sign. Uncle Martin did walking and advising. Len polished. We did the thing that looks like a ballet until it does not. Isla arrived at half nine to look and panic. The cup fell at ten, if time has any meaning. Delia called for a fix. Someone glued the handle on the wrong side. I wanted to shout. I did not. Then the siren."

Her voice had gone flat. Tessa let the silence cover it and made fresh tea because tea is the least intrusive balm human beings have managed to invent.

"I asked you earlier," Poppy said after a while, "for a letter. I did not ask your aunt because she would have given it without question and then I would have felt like I had cheated. I wanted one from Delia because she has the kind of name that makes desks nod."

"I would have written," Tessa said.

"I will take yours now, once all this is over," Poppy said. "I will pay you in tarts and the promise of quiet at your door. I am tired of having to ask people who like their power."

"You may have mine," Tessa said. "And the quiet."

Poppy looked at Bramble and exhaled again. "I know I am a suspect," she said, bald. "People like me who argue in cloakrooms become suspects. If you think I cannot feel that, you have never lived in a small place. I will not carry it alone. I will carry the part where I wanted something and did not get it and stomached a clever woman with a list. That part is mine. The rest can go to the person whose hand does not mind shoving."

"That is clear," Tessa said. "Inspector Shaw likes clear."

Poppy finished her tea and put the cup down on the coaster as if she were in church and the table was sacred. She stood, paced three steps, then came back, right hand worrying the ring on her index finger, left hand useless as a counterweight.

"What will you do now," she asked. "You and your eyes."

"I will take your statement to Inspector Shaw in the shape he prefers," Tessa said. "I will put down the time you placed the saucers and the way your hand holds a cup. I will write about the rehearsal and your argument and your right thumb with a smear of icing sugar that never seems to leave the cuticle. He will test the rail residue and listen to the crate. He will look at keys."

Poppy's mouth twitched. She glanced at her thumb and rubbed at the ghost of sugar with her right forefinger. "Fine," she said. "Write my thumb into your book."

"I already have," Tessa said, and closed her notebook to prove it.

They were interrupted by Mabel, who swept back in with a bag of scones and the air of a general pleased with a drill. She took in Poppy's face, the mugs, the set of the room, and handed over the paper bag without asking an unkind question.

"Cut these," she told Tessa. "We will all pretend butter is medicine."

Poppy sat again and ate as if her jaw had a job but not a taste. She put her half scone down in the exact centre of the plate with her right hand and brushed crumbs with her right. When she thanked Mabel she did it with her right hand around the cup again. The pattern repeating calmed Tessa's gut. Marks that line up are comfort.

"Do you know Vera," Poppy asked Mabel, as if practice in an older woman might explain a younger one. "I mean do you know her beyond the invoices."

"I know she hates mess and loves lists," Mabel said. "She looks at a room and sees the invoice in the air above it. That is a talent. It is also a set of blinkers."

"She looked at me like a speed bump," Poppy said. "Delia looked at me like an amateur. Between them they parked themselves on my chest."

Mabel nodded. "Between them they built a fine stage for a fall," she said, then softened it with a look. "And that is all I will say. The Inspector will prefer we feed him nouns and times rather than adjectives."

Poppy stood, appetite folded away. "I have to go to my mother's and sit at a table where Isla will pick at cake and my father will cut the slices too large because he is afraid small will look like giving up."

"Take the rest of the scones," Mabel said. "Tell them the library insisted."

Poppy laughed properly for the first time that day. "You are a menace in a cardigan," she said, and then sobered. "Thank you for seeing me and not treating me like a headline."

"We prefer footnotes," Tessa said. "They tell the truth without making a fuss."

Poppy took the paper bag in her right hand, the tote over her left shoulder, and paused at the door. "He would not have wanted it this way," she said. "Whoever did it. Whoever meant it or did not mean it. They would not have wanted to watch Isla carry that morning on her back."

"No," Tessa said. "But they may have wanted a different thing more."

Poppy nodded once and left with the bell marking the beat.

For a minute the shop held its breath. Mabel stood with her hands flat on the counter, palms mirroring grain. Bramble made a small throat sound that might have been a comment on human illusion. The kettle clicked again as if it had felt ignored.

"I do not like the way the village will lean on that girl," Mabel said. "She looks like a person who can take it, and people love to test that theory."

"She will have a letter from me," Tessa said, opening her notebook. "She will have a line in a statement that says what her hands do without thinking. And she will have a biscuit when she walks past my door."

"Write it," Mabel said. "Then we will send it."

Tessa turned to a clean page and wrote, at the top, Poppy Hartley, right handed. She wrote exactly what she had watched. Right hand lifts cup, stirs, signs, cuts, carries. Watch on left.

Icing sugar smear right thumb cuticle. Handle this morning left lean, left set, left proud. She added the rehearsal row in the cloakroom, the words about the loan, the refusal, the slammed door, the people present. She noted times. She noted that Poppy placed the saucers at nine forty, confirmed again.

She underlined right handed twice, then closed the book. "We will take this to Shaw," she said. "We will not turn it into opinion."

"Good," Mabel said. "He has enough of those delivered like flowers."

They stepped out into air that had forgiven the day for a minute. The walk to The Thimble & Fern was short enough to feel neighbourly. Shaw had perched again near the back window with his folders in a small fort. He looked up and read their faces as if they were memos.

"Ms Harper," he said. "Mrs Clegg. What do we have."

"Poppy's afternoon," Tessa said. She handed him the page she had copied in a second hand that morning for this purpose. "Right handed. The wrong handle was set left."

He read, pencil tapping once at the underlined words. "Thank you," he said. "I like it when facts remove drama. It narrows."

"She also confirms the rehearsal row," Mabel said. "And the loan refusal."

"Both already on my list," he said. "This gives them better shape. I appreciate the hand dominance. I prefer when things stand on more than gust."

He slid the note under his clip and looked past them to the door, where Vera had appeared like a thought someone wished to examine later. Vera spotted them and altered course slightly, as if to avoid conversation she could not control. Shaw's gaze returned.

"Anything else," he asked.

"Only a small request," Tessa said. "When you have the lab result on the rail residue, write it on paper before you call me. Phones forget the important bits."

"I will write it on paper," he said. "And then I will say it twice."

On the way back to Ivy Lane, Mabel tucked her hand in Tessa's elbow in the manner of women who have shared kitchens. "You are thinking about that cup again," she said.

"I am thinking that whoever set it left did not think about the bride's right hand," Tessa said. "They thought about shape and speed. They thought about photographs. They did not think about hands."

"Who are our left hands in this story," Mabel asked.

"Not Poppy," Tessa said. "Not Isla. Len writes with his right. Uncle Martin holds his pen in his right. Vera flips her clipboard in her left and writes in her right." She paused, remembering a photograph Ruth had taped to the Barn's back wall from a charity ball. A person trimming ribbon with a pair of shears in their left while the right steadied the coil. Vera again. Or another. Too early to fix.

She opened the shop and stood for a moment with her hand on the doorframe, an old superstition that had turned into a habit. Bramble went to his post under the shelf. Outside, the canal made its usual slow vow to get where it was going.

Tessa wrote one more neat line and slipped it under the glass beside the brass sketch.

Poppy right handed. Handle was wrong left.

Then she put on the kettle because there are days when the only honest next step is steam and a clean mug.

EIGHT

By early evening the village had tired itself into a hush. Ink & Ivy wore the kind of quiet that sits on the shoulders and tells them to drop an inch. Tessa put the Closed sign at a decisive angle, wiped the bench one last time, and slipped the two glassine envelopes into the small safe behind the till. The brass tab with its laurel stamp lay in her head like a coin under a tongue. The ledger stub with its broken "Phase 1" shaped the rest of her thoughts whether she invited it or not.

Bramble stretched, toes splayed, then sprang up as soon as she reached for his lead. Mabel tapped the bell with her knuckle on the way out and fell into step with them as if a small procession had always been planned. The air smelled of cut grass and baking, the two things most villages manage even on bad days.

"We will take the long loop by the hall," Mabel said. "I promised Lin I would look in on the lavender. He will have feelings about ribbons near stems."

"Lin always has feelings about stems," Tessa said. "And most things that shade them."

Fernvale Hall's garden sat brave and tidy under a sky that had gone the soft blue of crockery glaze. Evening made the lavender hum in a way that did not sound like bees. It sounded like a thousand small things doing work. The urns flanking the path looked less ceremonial now and more like the sensible idea they were, a way to keep people from standing where they had stood when the day went wrong.

Lin crouched beneath the nearest urn with secateurs and an eye like a plumb line. He was the sort of man who carried string in his pocket that matched his socks. His hat had the character of a loyal dog. He stood when he saw them and took off the hat with a nod that honoured grief without letting it swallow him.

"Evening," he said. "I was wondering whether you would come meddle."

"We prefer the term assist," Mabel said.

"I prefer results," Lin replied, pleased. "Hold this." He handed Tessa a tie of soft twine and pointed with his chin at the trailing ivy someone had coaxed down the post. "We do not want it to catch skirts tomorrow. Loop and tuck, please. No knots that will require a sailor."

Tessa looped and tucked. The tying put her shoulders level and her head clear. Practical tasks had saved worse days. Lin stepped back to approve, then turned his attention to the path.

"Len has been told not to polish anything that has a right to stay still," he said. "I think the Inspector made the point with sufficient poetry."

"Len heard him," Tessa said.

"Good," Lin said. "I like Len. I do not like his bucket when a planner is shouting pictures in his ear."

He cut a stem that had ideas about freedom and laid it gently in his trug. When he spoke again the words came as if they had been waiting.

"You know they ran a blackout last night," he said. "Not a power cut, before you ask. A rehearsal. Delia wanted ambience. The upper windows have those infernal dimmers on the skylights, so she begged for a full lights-out run. Candles. Fairy strings. The works."

"Blackout," Tessa repeated. "On purpose."

"On purpose," Lin said. "I was here to tell them where people would walk when they could not see their own shoes. Len muttered about timings and fuses and said he had a sheet for it. He loves a sheet when he can call it official."

"Where did he get the sheet," Mabel asked.

"The office," Lin said. "There is a whole drawer with forms no one fills and forms that keep the roof on. Health and safety keeps Len awake and rests him by turns. He had a printed schedule pinned to a clip. Outage test, he called it. Skylight dimmers path test, he said. Mains off for a one minute check, he said. Then a longer dim for the candle trial so the photographer could whinge in real time."

"How long for the longer dim," Tessa asked, light as if she were admiring his string.

"Six or seven minutes," Lin said. "He said the dimmers take a minute to cycle down and a minute back up and the rest in the middle was for candles and sighs. It was in the evening so no one fell over a toddler. He was rather proud of himself."

"The sheet exists," Tessa said.

"It exists," Lin said. "If Mrs Dray has not tidied it into a filing system that no one else can navigate. It had the times intended for tonight as well if the bride had wanted soft light at the first dance. They write these things now so everyone can blame the schedule. Progress."

Mabel snorted. "Progress does love a list."

Lin checked the level of a stake and frowned at a ribbon that had sagged a finger's width. He adjusted it. "They ran the blackout. It was Friday, half seven. I timed it in my head because I am my father's son. I walked the aisles with a torch. Delia wanted a fade to dark then candles like stars. Very poetic. I told her poetry has ankles."

"Anyone on the landing during the run," Tessa asked.

"Delia," Lin said. "Len. Vera drifted up to inspect a bow in the doorway because the woman cannot ignore silk. Martin did a speech about fire exits while holding his phone. The rest of us went into the hall proper and whispered like children in a bad film."

"Any problems," Tessa asked.

"Other than the obvious," Lin said. "The dimmers groaned. The mains went off cleanly and came back with no drama, which is how we like it. Someone tripped a tea light in the corner and I growled. Delia smiled at me as if she could tame gravity. She could tame many things. Not gravity."

Mabel crouched to pick up a fallen sprig and sniffed it. "Did the outage sheet come out again this morning," she asked. "Or was that only for last night's show."

"Len kept it on the clipboard," Lin said. "He meant to use it next week for the Harvest craft trial. There is a dimmer test every month now because someone thought skylights would modernise us. You cannot modernise a Georgian roof without trouble, but try telling that to a leaflet."

"Where does Len keep the clipboard," Tessa asked.

"In the office behind the door," Lin said. "Hook on the wall. He leaves it there so he sees it when he reaches for his cap and pretends he will not forget. The sheet had slots for start and stop, with boxes for initials. He loves an initial. He forgets to bring his pen."

Tessa looked past Lin toward the side door. Evening lit the corridor softly. The tape had come down from the landing but the numbered markers still stood like small tense tents. She felt the pull to go and see and fought it. Shaw had given her permission to look before. He had not given her permission to go collecting clues like an overconfident magpie. She settled for memorising the way the light fell along the rail where the cap had looked dulled this morning.

"Why did Delia want the blackout," Mabel asked. "Other than romance and photography."

"She said candles make people gracious," Lin said. "She said soft light means soft faces. She also said you could hide a good many sins in shadow. Those were her exact words. She had a laugh in them. I did not."

"You did not because you like ankles," Tessa said.

"I like people to see their feet," Lin said. "It saves me from writing letters to hospitals about gravel burns."

He trimmed another stem. His hands had that spare efficiency people's hands get when they have done ten thousand tasks that looked small and added up to a life. He stood and surveyed his work. "Tell your Inspector that if he wants the sheet I will happily testify to its neatness," he said. "If he wants a copy, I will watch him collect it. I do not put my fingers on paperwork without witnesses in a week like this."

"He will like you," Mabel said. "You make his job sound like a calendar."

"His job is a calendar," Lin said. "It is also noses in places that squeak."

He set down the secateurs and rubbed his thumb along the mark they always left on his finger. "You know what else I noticed," he said, the words coming as if he had not been sure whether they were worth saying. "When they did the fade, the skylights went grey, not dark. The dimmers make the roof feel like evening instead of night. Pretty. Useless for seeing. You brace your hand without thinking. People reach for the cap."

"The cap," Tessa said, quiet.

"I stood by the landing and watched Delia glide like a person in a perfume advert," Lin said. "She ran her palm along the cap once as if it were a banister in a dollhouse. It was a habit. She touched it every time she took the turn. You know when people do that little pat that says, this is mine. That."

He picked up his hat and settled it back on his head. "All right then," he said, brisk. "That is enough sad poetry. I have a border to straighten. The lavender needs manners. Go and write your notes, Ms Harper. And tell Len that if he comes near these stones with a mop I will bury the bucket where the fennel grows."

"We will pass on your love," Mabel said.

They left Lin to tell stems what to do and walked round to the side door. Len's office light glowed. He sat at his desk with his ledger open and his chin in his hand, a man trying to tame lists with gravity. When he saw them he rallied, then remembered himself and did not stand.

"I am not meant to let anyone rummage," he said before they could speak. "Inspector Shaw has me on a leash. If you wait, I will fetch what you ask for and hold it up at a distance like a used handkerchief."

"We would like to see your outage schedule," Tessa said. "The dimmers and mains test. Lin says there was a run last night."

"There was," Len said, relief softening the edge of his voice. "A thing that went right on a day that did not." He reached behind the door where a clipboard lived on a hook and lifted it down with both hands as if it had weight. He did not hand it to her. He held it up so she could read.

The top sheet had a printed header in brisk font. FERNVALE HALL ELECTRICAL SYSTEMS: LIGHTING OUTAGE AND TEST SHEET. Under it, boxes marched in order. Date, time start, time end, system, area, initials. A column on the right read Notes for caretaker. Someone had written in slot one: Fri, 19:32, 19:39, Skylight Dimmers, Main Hall, LP. Slot two: Fri, 19:41, 19:42, Mains Test, Hall Circuit A, LP. Slot three was blank. Below, a fresh day's grid began with Sat, and an empty line for any timed run a planner might have insisted upon. In Notes, a neat hand, not Len's, had written for slot one: Fade to candle trial per DP. In slot two: 60 sec cut. Test alarms silent.

"DP," Mabel said. "Delia's initials."

"Her maiden name still sits in people's fingers," Len said. "We never quite learn the new ones."

"May I copy the times," Tessa asked.

"You may say them out loud and see whether your mind prefers digits or breath," Len said, trying for humour and nearly making it. "I cannot let paper walk. I will never find my job again."

Tessa read them back softly. "Nineteen thirty two to thirty nine for the dimmer fade. Nineteen forty one to forty two for the mains test. That gives a window where the room expected dark."

"It does," Len said. "I did the torch check while they cooed."

"Anyone else carry a torch," Mabel asked.

"Vera pretended her phone is a torch," Len said. "Martin borrowed a light from the electrician on Thursday and never returned it. I suspect he thought it romantic to hold one like a guide. It is in his car now, shining quietly at his conscience."

Tessa kept her face still. "Thank you," she said. "That helps me understand how last night felt."

"It felt like trouble rehearsing," Len said. "And yes, I hear myself. I am an old man."

"You are a man who has mopped more trouble than most," Mabel said. "Which grants you prophecy."

Len flushed at that in a way that made him look younger, then remembered sorrow and went grey again. He hung the clipboard up with ceremony, as if putting it in a drawer would anger it, and closed his ledger as if one list per day was a mercy.

The corridor smelled faintly of polish and carnations. Tessa stood at the landing with her hands in her coat pockets and looked at the place where the cap had dulled. She kept her hands to herself. She pictured the fade. Skylights lowering the day to a patient grey. Candles blooming on the tables. The hall in the hush people make when they are pleased with an idea. A hand on the cap because the body knows where security lives. The same hand an hour later, when the landing shone and the cap had been wiped with something that made the varnish whisper.

"Enough," Mabel said, soft but firm. "He told you not to test. You are testing with your face."

"I know," Tessa said. She turned toward the door with effort.

At The Thimble & Fern, Detective Inspector Shaw had set up a temporary island of order in the back corner again. A laptop, two folders, a cup with a lid he distrusted but tolerated. He was using his pencil. The pencil remained his centre of gravity.

"Good," he said when he saw them. "I was about to come looking."

"Lin's feelings," Mabel said. "And Len's sheet."

Shaw looked interested enough to close his folder. "Explain."

Tessa told it clean and straight. Lin's account of the lights-out run. The skylight dimmers at nineteen thirty two. The mains test at nineteen forty one. The sheet on the clipboard behind Len's door with boxes for initials. The note in Delia's neatness about the candle trial. She did not add colour. She did not add the picture in her head of a hand running along a cap twice, once with varnish under it and once with a thin, clean drag. She trusted him to have his own pictures.

"Good," Shaw said. "That gives me something I can ask our electrician to love. I will collect the sheet. I will photograph and leave it. I will not start a war with Mrs Dray over filing. She wins such wars."

"She does," Mabel said.

Shaw wrote the times twice, once for his folder, once on a slip he tucked into his pocket. He tapped the pencil, then looked up. "Tell me how this helps you," he said to Tessa, which was his way of testing his own assumptions without making a fuss.

"It gives me a window," Tessa said. "It tells me last night they practised the muddle. If someone wanted a few minutes of slow sight at a known hour, they had it scheduled. If someone wanted to see how a person moved in dim, they could watch. If someone wanted to set a habit in a hand, they had time."

"Set a habit in a hand," he repeated, as if tasting it. "Interesting."

"It also tells me the dimmers make evening, not night," Tessa said. "People brace. They touch wood. They are more likely to leave a print at a cap."

"Which they did," he said. "Which my lab will tell me about in the morning."

He stood and stretched the way people do when they have been polite to their own spine for an hour. "The blackout rehearsal will interest me for timing," he said. "It will interest others for atmosphere. I will keep them separate."

Mabel nodded like a teacher whose pupil had remembered the point of a lesson. "Collect the sheet before Mrs Dray files it under 'Things the police will want on Tuesday'," she said.

"I am going now," he said. "If anyone asks what I am carrying, I will say biscuits."

"Bring actual biscuits," Mabel said. "It helps with Mrs Dray."

He left, pencil tucked behind his ear as if he had been born with it there. Tessa watched the door swing shut and felt the day settle into a slightly different shape. Timings did that. They turn fog into corridors.

They walked back to Ink & Ivy under a sky that had decided to be kind. Bramble trotted, pleased with his rank in the small pack. The canal reflected a single duck that took itself very seriously. At the shop, the bell made its small civil sound. The room greeted them with paper and resin and the quiet relief of things that do not change their minds.

Tessa poured tea and wrote two lines on her pad with care.

Outage sheet exists on Len's clipboard. Fri dimmer 19:32–19:39. Mains test 19:41–19:42. Notes in Delia's hand. Sat line blank.

She underlined exists. She added, smaller, Lin saw Delia run palm along cap during fade. Habit. She did not circle it. She did not want to love it too much too soon.

Mabel read over her shoulder, then reached for the biscuit tin with the gravity of a nurse. "You are thinking of the blackout as a rehearsal for something other than candles," she said.

"I am thinking it was a rehearsal for control," Tessa said. "Which is what candles are for anyway."

"You will make a good speech when the time comes," Mabel said. "Not yet."

"Not yet," Tessa agreed.

The bell chimed once more. Isla's mother stepped in with a tin that had seen service since weddings wore hats. She set it on the counter the way people set burdens down when they intend to lift them again later.

"The girls are home," she said. "We will breathe and eat tart and then breathe again. I came to say thank you for the cup and to tell you that the saucer has taken up residence at the Barn's back desk like a cat that does not know its address."

"It will be returned properly," Tessa said. "Inspector Shaw will see to it."

"Good," she said. "Delia would have insisted. She liked sets."

She looked at Tessa with the polite interest of a person who sees something in another's face and wonders whether a question would be rude. Then she decided against it and pushed the tin forward.

"Shortbread," she said. "For helping. For the dog. For the Inspector if he is polite."

"We will issue it as needed," Mabel said.

When the door had closed and the bell had run out of sound, Tessa stacked the day's new pieces on the mental table with the old ones. Citrus that cut varnish. A wrong-set handle that put the left in charge of a right-handed plan. A saucer that left the room before it could be photographed. A brass leaf with a hole for a ring. A stub that said Phase 1 in a tone taken from a brochure. And now a sheet with boxes that turned light into numbers and numbers into permission.

She opened her notebook and wrote one more line, then shut it as if that could keep the words from falling out.

Blackout rehearsed. Habit on the cap. Window exists.

NINE

Fernvale Community Barn kept its treasures in a tidy warren behind the shop floor, where the air smelled of paper, starch, and hope. A bell on a spring marked comings and goings with a cheerful ping that felt like a lie today. Gwen had pulled her hair back with a pencil and tied her apron on as if a knot could steady the room. Ruth sorted lamps with the concentration of a surgeon.

"We are back," Mabel announced, holding a tin as tribute. "Shortbread. Genuine. No raisins."

"Bless you," Ruth said. "We will eat after the next crisis."

Detective Inspector Shaw had reached the Barn before them and turned the back room into a small picture of order. He had three crates pulled against the wall under the sign that read INTAKE. The HALL MIXED crate from the morning sat open with a police label. Beside it, a smaller box bore a sharpie scrawl: LOCKE & LINEN OFFCUTS. A third box, plain and taped well, had a white slip pocket on the side where Gwen slid donor notes. Shaw stood with his pencil and his patience.

"Thank you for coming," he said to Tessa. "We will do this by sequence, not sentiment."

"Sequence suits us," Tessa said.

Gwen tugged on a blue glove like a person called to theatre. "I made a new rule," she said. "It is called do not consolidate when the police are in the building." She looked defiant and tired all at once. "It is a good rule. I wish I had made it at nine."

"You consolidated," Shaw said.

"I tidied," Gwen said, and winced at herself. "Which is another word for consolidated."

Ruth set her lamp aside with a sigh. "We were busy. The church sale men came to borrow tables and opinions. Dot tried to make the front look nice. I told her the back looks after itself. The back did not listen."

Shaw nodded at the smaller box. "Start with this one."

Gwen pulled the top open and eased back the flaps. Inside sat a neat stack of ribbon rolls and a bag of napkin rings. A handwritten card lay on top. Gwen lifted it with two fingers and handed it to Shaw. He read aloud.

"Locke & Linen, donation, offcuts and samples. Driver: G. Pike. 9:12, Saturday." He glanced at the pocket on the side of the box and slid out a second slip. "Barn intake slip, printed from your little machine. Logged at 9:13. Signature, G. Pike." He lifted his head. "Who is G. Pike."

"Gareth Pike," Ruth said at once. "Vera's Saturday driver. He calls everyone 'chief' and parks straight."

"Did he bring this through the front," Shaw asked.

"He brought it round the back," Gwen said. "He knows we prefer it. He knocked, I wheeled the trolley, he signed, I printed a slip because I like proof." She gestured to a battery-powered printer the size of a loaf on the shelf. It sat with a lead coiled around it, smug as a cat. "We print for large donors or people who argue. Locke & Linen argues only about cushions."

"Did you open this box at nine thirteen," Shaw asked.

"No," Gwen said. "I put it there to open later. I was busy with a woman who wanted to return a picture frame because her ex had put his face in it."

Shaw's mouth twitched. He set the slip back, then pointed to the white pocket on the third box. "And this."

Gwen pulled the pocket slip. "Hall clear, mixed, collected by Pete," she read. "Time stamp 10:55 because that is when I printed the label for tidy. He dropped it at 9:28 and frightened Dot. She wrote his name wrong again. He is not Peter. He is Pete." She peered closer. "I put the wrong time on the slip. Again. I need sleep."

"We have you on the bell at 9:28," Ruth said. "The bell terrified Dot and she stepped on a candlestick. She swore like a person whose toe had met a Victorian weapon."

Shaw pointed his pencil at the HALL MIXED crate. "This is the one where we found the saucer on top at noon," he said for the record. "Gwen, did you move anything from the Locke & Linen box into Hall Mixed."

Gwen's cheeks went pink. "I might have lifted one plate," she said. "If the top of one box looks like the top of another I put like with like. It is a sickness. I am trying to be better."

"Describe the plate," Shaw said.

"A saucer," Gwen said. "White, with a blue stamp. It sat on top because someone thought you cannot put plates under napkin rings. They were right. I put it on the Hall crate because I thought someone had moved it by accident and I was saving you time. You can throw me in jail. I will tidy."

Shaw did not throw her anywhere. He looked instead to Tessa. "The saucer you saw earlier."

"White," Tessa said. "Blue stamp. Hairline from two to four. A faint clear smear by the inner notch. You have it in your custody."

Shaw nodded once. He lifted a plastic wallet from his folder and slid out a printed photograph. "Taken at eleven forty-eight when we lifted it," he said. "Same hairline. Same smear. We have a shot of it on the Hall crate."

He tucked that away and then pointed to the Locke & Linen box again. "Did you, at any point, see that saucer in this box."

"I did not see it," Gwen said. "I moved it with the sort of muscle memory that has no business moving anything. It looked like the one on the Hall crate when I pulled the Hall crate out from the wall later." She pinched the bridge of her nose. "I am not sleeping tonight."

Ruth leaned against the table and folded her arms. "We do have one thing," she said. "Because we pretend to be modern. Dot likes to take a quick picture of what is in a donation box when people like Mr Pike turn up. She says it makes her feel like she is on a programme. We humour her. She uses a phone and the little printer and she prints one for the pocket because she likes evidence."

"Where is Dot," Shaw asked.

"In the stock room," Ruth said. "She is putting faces in frames for practice."

Gwen went to fetch her. Dot appeared from the stock room with a phone on a lanyard and a face that tried to be brave. She had a fringe that forgot to be neat and an earnestness that made Mabel soften on sight.

"We take little pictures," Dot said, already helpful. "Here." She scrolled deftly, then set the phone on the table and pointed. "This morning at nine twelve when Mr Pike dropped, I took a shot because the sun was pretty through the door. He laughed. I printed it for the pocket."

The photograph showed the open Locke & Linen box on the trolley. On top of the ribbon rolls lay a white saucer. Its hairline, delicate and familiar, glinted at the rim. In the corner of the frame a high-vis sleeve read LOCKE in block letters. The phone had stamped the time in the corner. 09:12.

Shaw's voice stayed level. "Print that, please."

Dot tapped twice. The little printer whirred. A small glossy picture slid out like a tongue. Dot handed it to Shaw with a look that said I did not know I could be useful.

"Thank you," he said, and meant it. He slid the print into a plastic wallet and wrote 9:12, Locke box, top layer. He did not underline. He did not need to.

Tessa kept her face still while her mind ordered its drawers. The chain now had a link that did not require anyone's memory. At 9:12, a box from Vera's warehouse sat on the Barn trolley with a saucer on top. At 9:28, the Barn bell rang for Pete with the Hall crate. By noon, the saucer sat on the Hall crate. Gwen had moved it because like belongs with like in a world that was not in the mood for rules. The intake slip on the Locke box said Gareth Pike at 9:12. The pocket on the Hall crate carried a slip printed later, but the bell had recorded the drop at 9:28. The fact placed the saucer with Locke & Linen before Delia fell.

Mabel breathed out through her nose. "That will cause conversation," she said.

"Everything causes conversation," Ruth said. "At least this one brings a photo."

Shaw looked at Dot. "Did Mr Pike say where the box came from."

"Warehouse," Dot said. "He said offcuts and samples for the Barn because Vera likes good publicity. He said we could put a picture on our board. I did not."

"Did he carry it himself," Shaw asked.

"He carried it to the trolley," Dot said. "I pushed. He called me chief. I gave him the slip to sign and he asked for a pen because he always pretends ours run out."

"Good," Shaw said. He wrote the name Gareth Pike, driver, 9:12, then tucked his notebook away. He turned to the box labelled Hall Mixed. "We will go through this layer by layer now with patience."

He did not rush. He photographed the top, then the next tier, one sheet of old newspaper at a time. Gwen hovered like a penitent. Ruth kept volunteers at the front from drifting back with questions. Mabel watched the doorway and sniffed at anyone who looked as if they might have an opinion to spare.

Tessa stood out of the way. She followed the work with her head rather than her hands. The layer under where the saucer had sat held council-issue white and two teacups chipped on the rims like old teeth. Beneath those, napkin rings. Beneath those, a curled length of ribbon that might have once been blush and now settled for romance. No second saucer with a blue stamp. No note tucked clever. Only the strange comfort of things that had belonged to different mornings and found themselves in the same box by chance.

Shaw paused at the ribbon. Tessa leaned in enough to see the edge. Not Vera's Lot 7B. The print had more yellow in the green and the wire had frayed. He replaced it and moved on.

At the end he closed the lid and wrote on the top in block letters: CONTENTS LOGGED. DO NOT MOVE. He peeled a strip of evidence tape and set it firm. He did the same to the Locke box after removing the ribbon rolls and the napkin rings to photograph the cardboard beneath. Nothing hid. He lifted a flap and sniffed, almost greedy for residue. If any scent of citrus lingered, the warehouse had kept it.

"Right," he said. "We have an intake photo of the saucer in the Locke box at 9:12. We have a bell record of the Hall crate at 9:28. We have the saucer on the Hall crate by eleven forty-eight. We will not now argue about whose memory deserves biscuits."

Gwen subsided into something like peace. Ruth took the printed picture from his hand and studied it with the attention she gave lamps. "That is the one," she said. "Look at the little line. I remember thinking it should be priced as a set if we were lucky and then not thinking again."

"You are allowed not to think again," Shaw said. "I am paid to think twice."

He wrote a short receipt for the photograph, signed it, and left it with Ruth. He bagged the print in a proper sleeve and slid it into his folder as if closing a story. Then he looked at Tessa.

"Tell me how this sits in your map," he said.

"It gives Vera a route," Tessa said. "Her driver brought a box with a saucer on top at nine twelve. The hall crate arrived at nine twenty-eight. If the saucer began in her box, it did not begin in the hall. Either someone at the warehouse swept a matching piece into a donation on a morning when matching mattered very much, or someone at the hall had a matching piece and put it into Vera's box before it left, or someone at the Barn swapped items between the boxes with a tidy hand and a tidy conscience."

"Gwen moved it at some point," Shaw said.

"Gwen moved like to like after both boxes were here," Tessa said. "She did not conjure the saucer. It had to begin in one set of hands and end in hers. The photo puts it in Vera's at nine twelve."

Mabel tipped her head. "Could Vera's driver have picked up a stray saucer at the hall and tucked it on top of his box before he signed."

"He would have had to stop at the hall first," Tessa said. "At nine twelve the hall was arranging nerves, but not yet in a shout. Len does not let drivers carry boxes out of the storeroom without a line in his book. Locke box says warehouse. Hall crate says Pete. The driver's sleeve says Locke at the Barn's door at nine twelve. My bet is the route went warehouse to Barn."

Shaw looked pleased without letting anything flap. "I will ask Mr Pike for his route," he said. "I will ask him which doors he used. I will ask him whether he knows the difference between a donation and an invoice." He turned to Gwen. "And I will ask you for a second photo. Print me the one where you think the sun is pretty through the door."

Dot printed another without waiting to be asked. Shaw took it, wrote Sun pretty, 9:12, top layer shows saucer, and slid it into his folder with a small smile that only a good label can elicit.

Gwen exhaled. "If Vera comes in here and says I am careless, I will push her into the lamps."

"You will not," Ruth said. "You will leave the pushing to people with uniforms and better shoes."

"Quite right," Mabel said. "We have scones."

Shaw closed his folder. "I will visit Locke & Linen next," he said. "I will be very boring about routes and labels. If anyone tries to hand me a brand statement, I will hand it back and ask about tape."

"Tape," Tessa echoed.

"Boxes leave patterns," he said. "So does tape. If Vera uses a particular reel to seal her offcuts, I will look at the edges. People who are fussy about their kit are fussy about everything. The warehouse will tell on them."

He went, Dot saluted with her printer, and Gwen pretended not to wobble with relief.

"Your shop always smells like clean paper," Ruth said to Tessa as if needing to say something that was not a confession. "I think I will come in next week and buy a notebook."

"Buy two," Mabel said. "It is a hard week. We will all need notes."

They walked back past the lavender and the notice board where the Laurel Trust had pinned a cheerful flyer for the Autumn Gala. The small handwriting at the bottom that read Too dear for local pockets had gained a second line. Someone had written Prove me wrong.

Ink & Ivy greeted them with the soft chime that insisted on

normal. Tessa set the kettle while Mabel opened the shortbread and made that face people make when they find butter behaving. Bramble settled under the shelf and went to toe-twitch sleep like a small soldier off duty.

Tessa wrote three precise lines without haste.

Barn back room. Locke & Linen box logged 9:12 by driver Gareth Pike. Dot's photo shows saucer on top, hairline at rim. Hall crate bell 9:28. Saucer later on Hall crate. Chain begins with Locke.

She underlined 9:12. She added, smaller, G. Pike route to confirm. Tape pattern at warehouse. Then she closed the book.

Mabel leaned and read upside down. "You think Vera packed it."

"I think someone in her building packed it," Tessa said. "If she knew, she is clever enough to say she did not. If she did not know, her box still gave the saucer a lift into history."

"Could be an accident," Mabel said, because fairness is a muscle.

"Accidents happen," Tessa said. "So does tidying. So does malice. The photo gives us a start. The reason will follow."

She set two cups on the counter, poured, and let the steam draw a line in the air that washed the room clean for a minute. Outside, a boy on a bike rang his bell and then rang it again for the joy of it. The day offered that small charm as payment for being difficult.

The bell chimed once more. Vera Locke stepped in, framed by the doorway like a person on a poster for efficiency. She paused when she saw Tessa and Mabel together behind the counter. She had not expected an audience.

"Ladies," she said. "I have come for a word with the Inspector."

"He is out," Mabel said lightly. "Collecting tape."

Vera's smile did not crack. "How poetic," she said. "If he prefers verse to invoices today I will try again in the morning."

She turned to go. Tessa said, in a voice that sounded like a compliment, "Your driver Gareth parks straight."

"He does," Vera said. "I keep him for that reason among others."

"And he delivers early," Tessa said.

"He delivers on time," Vera corrected, the way people do when they have built a life on that exact difference.

When she had gone the room held its breath for a count of three, then exhaled. Mabel broke the shortbread and handed Tessa a piece.

"You will not accuse her in public," Mabel said.

"I will not accuse anyone in public," Tessa said. "I will write numbers on paper and hand them to a man with a pencil. He will ask about tape and routes. He will let facts do the shouting."

"And we will keep our door open," Mabel said. "Because people will need to buy pens for lists."

"They will," Tessa said.

She looked up at the hatbox on the high shelf. The handle had dried firm. The seam held. Some things accept sense. Others require time and evidence. She took her tea to the window and watched the canal. A barge slid by, unbothered by anyone's timetable.

"Tomorrow," Mabel said.

"Tomorrow," Tessa agreed, and wrote one last line.

Saucer's morning begins at Locke. End of argument, start of reason.

TEN

Sunday morning put a clean shirt on Fernvale. The canal looked scrubbed. Even the bakery chalkboard had straightened its handwriting. Tessa locked Ink & Ivy, slipped her chalk tin into her bag, and walked up to the hall with Mabel and Bramble. She had rung Detective Inspector Shaw at eight, asked for fifteen careful minutes, and heard him say, in that dry voice, that she could have them under supervision, with no liquids, no polish, and no enthusiastic experiments.

Constable Hargreaves waited at the door like a bookmark. "Inspector says I am the eyes," he said. "You are the hands. If anything looks like theatre I cough loudly."

"Cough early," Mabel said. "We are not here to audition."

Len let them in, grateful and wary at once. He had moved through grief into the part of sorrow that wears a list. "I have not touched a thing," he said. "I even told Mrs Dray to leave her feather duster at home. It nearly cost me a limb."

The landing looked smaller without tape but larger for what it knew. The numbered tents had gone. In their place, a hush lived between the top stair and the newel cap. Morning showed the floor's spiral of buffing with clarity. Len had stopped short of the cap yesterday. The swirl ended in a pale crescent of duller wood near the rail. The skid mark that had been tented now showed faintly as a darker path, a long sigh on the shine.

"Rules," Hargreaves said, holding up a palm. "Tell me what you intend."

"Mark the geometry," Tessa said. "Chalk only, dry, on paper or tape, no touching the cap. Then a controlled shoe test on a sacrificial strip that never leaves the flat."

He nodded. "Proceed."

Tessa opened her tin. Tailor's chalk, white and blue. She took two rolls of low tack drafting tape from her bag and a small fold of baking parchment that would take chalk like a breath and lift without sulking. She crouched and laid a run of tape a hand's width back from the stair edge, parallel with the nosing. She laid a second run along the outer edge of the landing, a gentle curve that matched the banister foot. In the middle she taped down a strip of parchment, corner to corner, the kind of pale that photographs well and remembers pressure.

She powdered the parchment with a whisper of chalk and blew once. The dust lay even, a shallow drift. Mabel stood as a screen against any sudden breeze that might get ideas. Len watched with the devotion of a man who has seen floors abused and was prepared to like this.

"Baseline," Tessa said. She took from her bag three pairs of shoes borrowed with permission from the lost property box and from Mabel's never-throw-away drawer. One, a soft rubber soled trainer, sole fresh, tread shallow. Two, a smooth leather men's lace-up with the kind of polish that loves to slide. Three, a low block heel, leather sole, toe slightly rounded, the sort bridesmaids choose when they have to stand for hours and still look like elegance.

"No one steps near the edge," Hargreaves said, voice even. "If you overreach, I cough first and catch second."

"Agreed," Tessa said.

She put on the trainer and walked the landing from the far wall to the tape, steady, a natural gait. The chalk on the parchment took her sole in a clean transfer with no smear. Where rubber met chalk, the dust made a print like a map. No drift. No drag.

She changed into the smooth lace-up and walked the same line with the same pace. The leather took chalk, slid a fraction, then stopped before the tape. The smudge at the leading edge was a fingernail's width. Mabel marked the toe tip on the tape with a pencil, a neat dot. "No drama," Mabel said.

"Now the block heel," Tessa said.

She took three practice steps on the safer wood behind the parchment, feeling for the landing's mind. Then she walked the line. The heel sounded honest. Chalk caught at the toe, smudged lightly, then held. Again, no drift of note. If a person misjudged on the flat, their foot corrected before the stair. If a person misjudged at the lip, the chalk would show at the nosing.

"Edge test," Hargreaves said. "No body near the descent."

Tessa kept both hands on the rail support, feet a safe width from the top stair. She placed the block heel at the tape, sole flat, then rocked the toe forward to mimic a poor step at the edge. The parchment took a harsh drag at the forward arc, a darker swipe that started at the line of tape, not before. She did not go beyond the lip. She lifted away.

"Mark it," she said.

Mabel pencilled a second dot and a small curve on the tape. Two signatures lived there now. One for a natural stride. One for a misstep at the brink.

"Now for what is bothering you," Hargreaves said. He had seen the line Tessa had been looking at since she entered, the faint dark on the floor that cut the buff spiral at a diagonal.

"Now for what is bothering me," Tessa agreed. "I will not step. I will trace."

She took the blue chalk and, without touching the wood, hovered along the darker line at a distance, sketching the path on the parchment by eye. The faint floor mark began well before the top stair, five hand spans back from the nosing. It ran straight, more straight than a trip allows, then kissed the tape line, then vanished where steps began.

She set the tip of the blue chalk at the first visible start, then measured with her own shoe as a unit. "Forty centimetres," she murmured. "Give or take the thickness of a temper."

"Meaning," Hargreaves said.

"Meaning if a person slipped because a toe caught the top stair, the slide signature begins at the edge," she said. "The drag begins where foot meets nosing. We just saw it. If a person slid before they reached the edge, you see a lead in on the flat, a loss of purchase where there is no stair yet, then the run carries the body to the lip. That is what this darker path says. A start on the flat, not at the drop."

"Because the floor was slick," Len said, voice small. "Because I covered it in pride."

"Because the floor was slick," she said, and did not soften it. "And because something on the cap took purchase from a palm that might have steadied the body. The two together make the slide."

Hargreaves crouched to see the blue trace on the parchment alongside the smears from the trainer, the leather, and the heel. He was not sentimental about chalk. He had the look of a man who likes a visible story. "So not a toe over a lip," he said. "A push on the flat."

"Or a sharp unbalance," Tessa said. "A body urged forward at the shoulder or spine, a railing that does not help, a floor that does not forgive."

He stood and looked at Len without sharpness. "The buffer alone might make a person cautious," he said. "The buffer plus a hand that fails is something else."

Len nodded, sick with agreement. "I know it," he said. "I knew it last night, and I know it more now."

"Let me finish the picture," Tessa said.

She rose, stayed well away from the edge, and breathed in near the cap without laying a finger on it. Yesterday's dull patch had dried further, but the air above the wood still held a note. Not furniture lemon. Not wax. Sharper. Peel. It sat at the back of the nose and made the world ring for a second, the way a true citrus does when it meets varnish.

"It is still there," she said. "Faint, but there. The citrus that takes a sheen away rather than giving it."

Hargreaves leaned in, careful not to huff over evidence, and sniffed once. He squinted. "I believe you," he said. "I am a poor nose. I smell polish too often. This is peel with a bite."

"Len's blend sits warm," Tessa said. "This sits thin and quick. Vera's No. 12 in her caddy smelled like this when uncapped."

Hargreaves wrote that down without comment. He had been told about the bottle by Shaw already. He drew a small map in his notebook, a rectangle for the landing, a dotted line for the skid, a cross for the cap. He measured the distance from Tessa's blue chalk start to the tape with a pocket rule and wrote 0.40 m. Then he wrote, in plain pencil, slide begins before lip.

"Enough," he said. "Lift the parchment."

Tessa peeled the tape slowly and rolled the chalked paper onto itself. No dust escaped. She held the roll like a scroll and passed it to Hargreaves. He slipped it into a plastic sleeve with the practised neatness that keeps lab techs in a good mood. He sealed it and wrote the room, the date, the time, and Tessa's name as observer.

"Thank you," he said. "You have stayed inside the fence. Inspector Shaw will prefer that."

"Tell him I admired the fence," she said.

Mabel did not move. She was looking at the banister cap as if she could see the moment overlaid there. Not the fall itself. The push. A hand at a shoulder. A second hand on wood that offered less grip than it should. Her jaw shuffled the thought into its proper place. She turned to Len.

"You are not a murderer," she said. "You are a man whose pride can be used by someone else. You will still write letters of apology in your head for twenty years. That is unavoidable. But it was a push."

Len took that in and did not weep. "I will oil every door in the church for a year," he said, earnest. "It will not fix a fall. It will keep guilt from eating me alive."

"Good plan," Mabel said.

They left the landing tidy, tape lifted, chalk captured. Hargreaves locked his evidence sleeve in a bag that had three zips and the authority of chain of custody. He walked them down the corridor and paused at the office door.

"Stay a second," he said. "There is a thing you might as well smell, since we are in the business."

On Len's desk, beside the sad tin of coins, lay a folded note on Locke & Linen card. Tessa recognised the neat, ruled hand. Spare set returned, 11:55. The card already sat on Shaw's list. Hargreaves did not point to it. He pointed to the hook board.

Spare B's screw was bare, its teapot shadow still clear. Only now a second arc of clean behind the screw showed, lower and smaller, where a different fob had knocked for a while and then gone. It looked recent. The dust had not found it yet.

"Someone has been playing musical hats," Mabel said. "People cannot resist tin teapots."

"They resist signing more," Hargreaves said. "Inspector says the locksmith will be able to tell me whether one of these keys has had a cousin cut recently."

"Ask about novelty blanks," Tessa said. "The teapot shapes come as keyrings, but festival stalls sell blank blades with silly tops. Someone with a sense of humour and a door to open would not resist."

Hargreaves made a note and snapped the bag closed. "We are done," he said. "Thank you for letting me cough only once."

"You coughed in your head," Mabel said. "I felt it."

He smiled, small and private, and saw them to the door.

Outside, the day had lifted into a blue that encouraged people to forgive the week. Tessa walked the path past the urns and paused halfway down the steps. She pictured the last two paces of a person surrounded by candle plans and ribbon. The push would not need to be vicious. A weight shift, a firm palm between shoulder blades, a body already off balance because the cap was less help than usual. If the person at the shoulder knew the dimmer's trick with light, all the better. Hands reach for rails in grey.

"You are writing narration in your head," Mabel said.

"I am writing a sentence for Shaw," Tessa said. "I will strip out the adjectives."

They stopped at The Thimble & Fern for fifteen minutes of information. Shaw sat at a corner table with his pencil, two cups of tea, and the face of a man who did not sleep long but slept well enough to outrun the worst of the night.

Hargreaves handed over the sleeve with the chalked parchment and the notes. Shaw read, wrote 0.40 m again in his own hand, and underlined before. He asked no questions for a full thirty seconds. He did not need to.

"Good," he said at last. "That says push to a jury without me threatening them with physics. If the cap residue sings citrus and not Len's kitchen lemon, and if the saucer began its morning in a Locke box, and if the keys have done what keys always do, then we are more than halfway from accident to act."

"You will ask Vera about routes again," Tessa said. "And about wipes."

"I will," he said. "I will also ask Mr Hale for his messages sent in the last week that contain the phrase single source. People write themselves into corners."

He folded the parchment sleeve as if it were a letter and slid it into his folder.

"I am going to the warehouse," he said. "You will go home. If you feel clever, make tea. If you feel restless, sweep your step. Do not chase anyone with a bottle of citrus and call it method."

"I will behave," Tessa said.

"Good," he said. "Because the next time you go near that landing I will have put a sign on it that reads Ms Harper may not chalk without an officer present."

"I enjoy an audience," she said.

He snorted, then sobered. "Thank you," he said, simple and true.

Back at Ink & Ivy, Tessa stood at the repair bench and laid her pencil beside her notebook. She wrote three lines that did not dress themselves up.

Parchment test shows skid signature begins on flat, approx 0.40 m before nosing. Edge misstep mark differs, begins at lip. Cap still holds faint citrus peel note.

She added, smaller, push, not stumble. Then she closed the book and set her pencil down with the quiet satisfaction of someone who had given a fact its best chance.

Bramble sighed and thumped his tail once. He had discovered a sun patch near the window and was lying in it with the air of a dog who took credit for weather. Mabel put the kettle on and tested one scone to make sure it was not lying. Outside, the canal moved with the patience of anything that has seen more than one mystery and refuses to rush.

"Next," Mabel said.

"Next we wait for the lab to hum the cap," Tessa said. "And for tape to tell the truth at the warehouse."

"And for a person to feel the ground tilt under their feet," Mabel said.

"They will," Tessa said. "Gravity keeps its promises."

ELEVEN

Sunday brought a polite light to The Thimble & Fern. People came in for coffees they did not need and left them half drunk because they wanted to look useful in public. Shaw had taken the back corner again, the same pencil, the same folders, the same steady weather. Mabel held the fort at the counter with a biscuit tin and a look that warned off theory.

Bramble lay under Tessa's chair as if assigned to guard ankles. He thumped his tail once when the bell chimed and Vera Locke arrived with a navy folder and the walk of a person who never met a queue she could not make shorter.

"Inspector," she said, crisp. "You asked for proof. I bring proof."

"Let us see it," Shaw said. He did not offer the theatre of a greeting. He offered a flat table.

Vera placed the folder down and opened it with neat hands. Inside, a printed manifest clipped square; beneath it, a card slip from a fuel pump; beneath that, a photocopied page from a delivery ledger with a highlight where she wanted the eye to go.

"This is my Saturday," she said. "Locke & Linen van two. Gareth Pike driving. Manifest entries printed at eight, signed as completed by the driver on return. You will see the Fernvale drop was ribbon supplements and a spare cloth. After that, a short hop to Broadoak to swap a tablecloth someone mismeasured. Then fuel at Collymere Services because the tank was low. Then I met Mr Hale at eleven thirty to discuss your Trust's sponsorship pack wording. These are not ideas. These are times."

Shaw took the manifest first. The grid wore its columns like armour. 08:55 Load complete, L&L2 GP. 09:45 Fernvale Hall, ribbon box B, spare cloth 8ft. 10:15 Depart Fernvale. 10:27 Broadoak Barn, swap 8ft to 6ft. 10:43 Depart. 10:54 Collymere Services, fuel. Each entry had Gareth Pike's initials in a slanted hand, then, lower down, in a neat second hand, the word reconciled.

"Who writes reconciled," Shaw asked without looking up.

"I do," Vera said. "I reconcile stock and fuel against miles and returns. Drivers initial their times. I balance the sheet at day's end. It is how money fails to go missing."

He slid the manifest aside and examined the fuel slip. Collymere Services. Pump 4. 10:54. 31.7 litres. Card suffix 0017. A little logo in the corner announced the brand with cheer it had not earned. The time sat in a digital font that always looked a bit wrong.

"Cashier name," Shaw said.

"Self-serve," Vera said. "Fleet card."

He turned to the photocopied page. A van checklist. Tyre pressure. Lights. Wipers. A driver signature across a box marked return, 12:03. The signature matched the initials: GP written as if it had somewhere else to be.

Shaw made no sound of belief or disbelief. He wrote two times in his pad. 10:54 fuel. 11:30 meeting with Hale.

"What time did the call for the ambulance go out," Vera asked, pre-emptive.

"Eleven oh nine," Shaw said.

"Then at eleven oh nine I was not at your landing," she said. "I was between jobs. I would have been on the ring road or pulling into Collymere's slip road depending on whose clock you trust. The van's dash camera can be checked. Its card shows the doors opening at the pump. My driver signs a key fob out and in. You will have logs if you want logs."

Tessa watched her without blinking. The citrus note lived near Vera again, faint but faithful. The caddy smell had become a signature. She looked at the fuel slip without touching. The receipt font had that odd thinness some tills carry when their ribbon needs changing. The seconds were not printed. Only hours and minutes. She filed that away alongside a small memory that Collymere's wall clock in the kiosk liked to lag after power cuts.

Shaw turned the manifest back to the Fernvale line. "Nine forty-five at the hall," he said. "How long did you remain."

"Until ten fifteen," Vera said. "I corrected the banner drop, replaced a tablecloth, and told Len to leave the sign in the lobby because it spoils photographs. He moved it. If you hear that sentence four times today it will sound like confession. It is not. It is a housekeeping preference."

"You then went to Broadoak," he said.

"For a cloth swap," she said. "Nobody in Broadoak cares about this case. They will give you the time in the tone of someone who wants you to leave their bunting alone."

"You met Mr Hale at eleven thirty," he said. "Where."

"In his office," she said. "He wanted language for the sponsorship pack that did not make his trustees look hungry. I said hungry is better than needy and wrote him three phrases that sound like bridges. We drank his poor tea. I left at eleven forty-seven because one must pretend to have Sundays. Then I came home and ironed my cuffs."

She delivered all this while keeping her eyes level and her body still. If she lied, the lie wore tailoring. Tessa looked at the manifest again and saw one detail she did not love. In the row for Fernvale, the time Depart Fernvale read 10:15 in Gareth's hand. In the right-most column where Vera had written reconciled, someone had put a tiny dot above the one, an ink speck you would not see unless you stared. Not a correction so much as a ghost. She stored it and looked away so she would not test it with her eyes.

Shaw tapped the fuel slip. "Collymere is twelve minutes from Fernvale by van if you drive like a person with an insurance policy," he said. "By that route, at eleven oh nine you could be within three minutes of the pump or three minutes from the ring road."

"And still not on your landing," Vera said.

"True," he said.

Mabel cleared her throat softly and slid a coaster toward Vera's cup even though Vera had not asked for tea and did not intend to drink any. "We like furniture to keep its varnish," she said.

"I like it not to bloom under flash," Vera replied. "We have that in common."

The bell chimed. Martin Hale came in as if he had been rung for. He wore Sunday tidy and the confidence of a man who had chosen a tie before breakfast. He saw Vera's folder and smiled his committee smile.

"Ms Locke," he said. "Inspector. Ms Harper. Mrs Clegg. I promised my secretary I would avoid work on a Sunday. I am here because I am bad at promises."

"Mr Hale," Shaw said. "At eleven thirty yesterday were you in your office with Ms Locke."

"Yes," Martin said. "We discussed sponsorship tiers and whether the phrase 'single-source' frightens donors. She nixed it and told me to say 'trusted partners' instead. I wrote it down because I know a lifesaver when I hear one."

"How long did she remain," Shaw asked.

"Seventeen minutes," Martin said, without checking anything. "I had a call at eleven forty-seven and she left as I picked up."

"Did she leave by Canal Gate or the front," Shaw said.

"Front," Martin said. "She hates our back stairs. I do as well."

He was smooth without being oily, which Tessa always found more dangerous. He looked at Vera the way a sponsor looks at a vendor he would prefer to keep happy. She thought of the memo and the borrowed language and the way the council had fed his phrases back to him with pride. She thought of the glossy sponsorship board that would need exactly the words he had asked her to read.

Shaw wrote eleven thirty to forty-seven. He wrote front exit. He did not draw any arrows. He set the pencil down and let his eyes rest on the fuel slip again as if willing it to confess ambition. It did not.

Vera said, "If you are done treating me as a suspect, I have a warehouse to run. I am sad about your planner. I am not the villain of this story. I brought ribbon and a receipt and a list. Unlike most stories, this one prefers the person with paper."

Shaw did not bristle. He never did. He simply leaned back a degree, the way a person shifts when they have filed an item under Not Top Of List For The Next Hour. Tessa felt the shift like a draught.

"Thank you, Ms Locke," he said. "We will speak again."

"You will," she said. "You like to tidy as much as I do."

She closed her folder and left with that starched slipstream in her wake. Martin stayed. He looked at the manifest as if checking whether it would stain his fingers.

"You will have our logs for keys by tomorrow," he said. "I have Sian pulling the sign-out sheets we pretended to keep. It will not be pretty. You may write us a fit-for-purpose note if you wish. Trustees love notes that say fit-for-purpose."

"I will write a different note," Shaw said. "It will say 'write things down'."

Martin smiled with the grace of a man who knew he deserved that. "I hear you," he said. "Do let me know if you need language for your press update. We have a decent press list. You might as well use it."

"We will not," Shaw said. "But thank you."

Martin nodded, shook hands, and left a faint scent of office and river stone where he had set his palm on the table to rise. The bell closed behind him with a neutral ring.

Shaw watched the door a second, then returned to the fuel slip. "Ten fifty four," he said. "Enough to cause me nuisance."

"You are leaning away," Tessa said.

"I am leaning," he said. "Away for the next hour. Toward someone else until something better knocks. Alibis throw their weight until you find the seam."

"The seam," Mabel said, dry. "Appropriate in a week with ribbon."

Shaw slid the manifest back across the table, not as a gift, as a courtesy. "Ms Harper," he said, "what bothers you."

"The receipt clock," Tessa said, and watched his eyes sharpen again. "Collymere's clock on the kiosk tends to drift. It lagged by four minutes after the last storm. They do not plug the printer into the same source as the wall clock, but if you want to anchor exact minutes you will want a second timepiece to argue with. Also, Gareth's initials say depart Fernvale at 10:15. If that is true, he did an in-and-out with Vera and was gone fifteen minutes before the shout. If it is aspirational rather than true, the fuel time carries more weight. But the fuel slip only has minutes, not seconds."

"Good," Shaw said. He wrote calibrate Collymere clock. He added dashcam check. "What else."

"Manifest reconciliation in a second hand," she said. "Hers. Fine. Expected. Still, it tells you nothing but that she is neat and likes it when things add up."

"What bothers you most," he asked.

"The fact that the saucer sat on top of her box at nine twelve with a driver's sleeve in the frame," Tessa said. "If she did not know then, someone in her building did. If she knew, she will say she did not. Either way, her box gave that saucer a lift out of the hall before the fall. The rest of her morning can be cut and clocked till tea. The first act sits in her yard."

"First act," Mabel echoed.

"We will keep that phrase," Shaw said. "It is tidy." He gathered the papers, tucked them, then stood. "I am going to confirm the kiosk clock and Gareth Pike's route. Then I am going to Martin Hale's office to ask for his call logs around eleven forty-seven and everything he typed with the words single source in the last week. That last part will irritate him. I will enjoy it."

He left them with the corner of the table still warm and a brief quiet that made the rest of the room louder by contrast. A couple at the far end abandoned their conversation about jam to talk about alibis in general, as if they had ever needed one for anything but cake.

Mabel topped up Tessa's tea. "Setback," she said, frank.

"Setbacks are kitchens," Tessa said. "You keep moving your hands until the pastry shows you a sign."

They took the long way to the canal because walking did what tea could not. At the corner, the notice board still wore the Laurel Trust flyer with its promise of a gala. Someone had added a second small line under Prove me wrong. It read Bring your own chair.

"True economy," Mabel said.

They crossed the bridge and leaned on the rail long enough to listen to the water make its old argument with the pilings. Tessa let her head replay Vera's timings until the edges dulled. Ten fifteen, depart. Ten twenty-seven, Broadoak. Ten fifty four, fuel. Eleven thirty, office. Eleven forty seven, call. Shaw had written eleven oh nine for the 999 call. None of that put Vera on a landing at the exact minute a push became gravity. All of it left her near enough to smell the hall if she wanted to.

Back at Ink & Ivy, the hatbox sat high and good, the seam held, the handle behaved. Tessa wrote three lines and left the adjectives on the floor.

Vera shows manifest and 10:54 fuel slip, Collymere. Martin confirms 11:30–11:47 office meet. Shaw cools on Vera. Note Collymere clock drift, minutes-only receipt, reconcile in V's hand.

She added, smaller, saucer still began at Locke. Then she tucked the page under the counter glass beside the brass leaf sketch and the dot for 0.40 m.

The bell chimed. Gareth Pike himself stood in the doorway with a hat he had not intended to remove and a face that wanted to be anywhere else. He held a folded paper in hands that were cleaner than his shirt.

"Inspector's at the yard," he said. "He asked me to bring this to you because you are his bard or something." He looked embarrassed. "He said you like paper."

"What is it," Tessa asked.

"A copy of the dashcam frame at the pump," Gareth said. "It shows my van nose to Pump 4 at ten fifty four with a bit of my jacket sleeve in the top corner because I am a gifted photographer. He said you would want to measure the shadow and tell him whether the clock is cuckoo."

Mabel clapped once, happier than she had any right to be about a shadow. "We have a ruler," she said. "And tea."

Gareth relaxed a fraction. "Tea wouldn't be wrong," he said. "It has been a morning."

The print showed the van's bonnet with the Collymere shop windows reflected in the paint, Pump 4's sign, and a strip of sky with a cloud that had the grace to take up a measurable amount of space. In the upper left the station's digital clock read 10:54. In the lower right, the dashcam's timestamp read 10:56:19.

Tessa set the ruler against the cloud's edge and the pump pole, not because the cloud mattered but because the angle made the reflection tell the truth. She liked to make two clocks speak to one another. She wrote 10:56:19 camera, 10:54 kiosk and underlined the gap. Then she poured Gareth tea and gave him a biscuit that had not lied yet.

"Tell the Inspector," she said, "that his kiosk clock loses two minutes and nineteen seconds to the dashcam on this morning. He will want his own version of that sentence in his own notebook. He can still like the fuel slip. He should not marry it."

Gareth blinked. "I do not know what that last bit means," he said cheerfully. "I only know I prefer being told I was at a pump to being told I was on a landing."

"You were at a pump," Mabel said. "Have another biscuit."

When he had gone, Tessa tucked the print under glass with the others. The corner of the counter had become a small, stubborn museum: a brass leaf, a torn ledger stub, a saucer's time, a blue chalk line, and now two clocks agreeing they did not agree.

Shaw returned at noon, a little thinner with effort and a little sharper with satisfaction. He tapped the glass lightly with a knuckle.

"Your cloud agrees," he said. "I will not marry the fuel slip. I will acknowledge it and go on a few dates with the dashcam."

He turned the pencil once in his hand. "I am still leaning away from Vera," he added. "Not forever. For this half day. Martin can enjoy the reprieve. He will not enjoy it long."

"Because of his phrases," Mabel said.

"Because of his phone," Shaw said. "He makes calls when people fall. The time says more than his voice. And his office printer says Phase One more often than a man should."

He left again. The bell did its civil work. Tessa stood very still for a moment, letting the day's new weight find its shelf. Then she wrote one more small line, the kind you do not read aloud.

Setback noted. Wall built of paper. Look for a loose brick.

TWELVE

Ink & Ivy's back room held the kind of quiet that lets decisions behave. The big window faced the yard, light fell true across the bench, and everything smelled of paper and the small clean of cotton thread. Tessa laid a wax cloth over the surface and set out four small glass jars, a pad of lint-free squares, and a notebook. She tied her hair back without thinking. Bramble settled by the door with the patience of a clerk keeping an eye on the corridor.

Mabel appeared with the kettle from the little sink and two mugs that had kept worse days upright. "Tell me what rule I am helping you follow," she said.

"No touching the hall," Tessa said. "Plenty of touching in here."

On the shelf above the bench sat the shop's half-forgotten chemistries. She pulled down a bottle of simple lemon oil she kept for customers who refused to let old wood be old, a tiny sample of generic citrus adhesive remover from a trade catalogue, and her own beeswax blend she made on slow Thursdays for frames that want kindness. Then she opened the bottom drawer and took out a small, unopened bottle with a dull white label. The code printed in faint grey read CB12-PEEL. Last winter's trade fair had sent a pack of samples. She had kept them tucked away because her bench rarely needed solvents with views.

Mabel clocked the label. "Your nose has been waiting for that one," she said.

"It has," Tessa said.

She put on gloves and marked the jars on the base, not the side, with a number one to four. She did not say which was which. Into Jar 1 she placed a folded cotton square and added three drops of lemon oil. Into Jar 2, a square with a skim of her own wax cut with a breath of white spirit. Jar 3 got two drops of generic orange goo remover from the catalogue. Jar 4, two drops of the CB12-PEEL she had not yet met anywhere but in Vera's kit and her own mind.

She capped each jar, shook it once gently to coat the square, then set them in a line. Mabel shuffled the order without ceremony and wrote the new sequence on a scrap only she could see.

"Blind," Mabel said. "I will heckle if you cheat."

Tessa cracked the lid on the first jar and drew in a slow, clean breath. Warm lemon and furniture, a fat note that sits in a room and tells you it meant to be there. She wrote warm, sweet edge, wood feeds. Jar two offered beeswax and paraffin with a faint whisper of spirit, the kind of scent that gets into hands and never quite leaves. She wrote honest wax, soft, not sharp.

Jar three lifted the back of her nose. Orange over something industrial, quick and a little rough. She wrote orange top, solvent under, slight throat grit. Jar four walked in like a bell. Peel, not perfume. Bright pith, bitter flick, then gone. It left no sweetness. It made the air ring a fraction and then let it go.

She didn't speak for a moment. Mabel watched her watch herself.

"Which is which," Mabel asked.

Tessa tapped the jars in order on the bench. "Lemon oil. My wax blend. Catalogue orange. CB12," she said. "If I'm wrong I will go home and pack."

Mabel turned the scrap. "Correct," she said, then reached for Jar 4 herself, cautious. She sniffed, blinked once, and put the lid back on. "That one bites and then leaves," she said. "I have met people like that."

Tessa smiled despite herself. "Now we see what they do to varnish."

She brought out a strip of old picture frame moulding she kept for tests, varnished oak with a good even finish. She cut it into four rectangles with the miter saw, labeled the backs A to D, and taped them to the bench so they would not skate. She marked out small squares on each with low-tack tape to keep the tests clear.

"Cotton swabs, one pass only," she said. "No scrubbing. Wipe and wait."

Mabel took the role of caller. "A," she said.

Tessa lifted the lid on Jar 1, dipped a clean swab, and drew it across the taped square on block A with a single, light pass. The finish took the oil and grew a gloss. It looked richer in seconds and smelled domestic.

"B," Mabel said.

Jar 2's swab left a softening with the slightest haze that would buff if invited. It looked like care, not change.

"C."

The catalogue orange hit the varnish and lingered. It left a slight matte smear that refused to make up its mind, a petulant shine that muddied the light until it dried. It also left a citrus parfum that overstayed.

"D."

She opened Jar 4. Even capped, the air above it had that bevelled edge her head recognised with a small, involuntary flinch. She drew a thin, neat pass across block D and stepped back. The line went dull almost at once, not cloudy, just less. The raggedness a camera flash loves. No residue. No oil. No perfume beyond the first flick.

"Light," Mabel said, moving the bench lamp to rake across the surface. Under the low angle the strip on D showed clean dulling and nothing else. A finger, if given leave, would find less grip there for a moment. The square on C was still messy, the one on A looked like polished honesty, and B asked for a buff and a biscuit.

Tessa wrote what she saw. Lemon oil enriches, sits. Wax softens, buffs. Catalogue orange smears, slow off. CB12 flashes, dulls cleanly. She added, cap note sharp peel, no sugar. Then she closed her eyes and stood with the cap at the hall, not touching, breathing that faint ring of pith and quickness. The memory landed without fidgeting.

"It is the same," she said quietly. "The banister cap yesterday. It wore this exact bite for a breath. Not lemon. Not orange. Not Len's wax. This."

Mabel didn't clap or sigh. She picked up Jar 4, turned it in her fingers, and read the tiny code near the hinge. CB12-PEEL. The lid had that little pin-prick spout under the cap, the sort that leaves a dot if you forget to wipe it. Vera's bottle had worn the same hinge smear.

"Memory cheats when it wants to be right," Mabel said, playing the part she always played. "Tell me what would make you doubt yourself."

"If the hall had been full of anything else citrus," Tessa said.

"It was not. Len's blend sat warm. No one boiled oranges. The florist's table behaved. The only sharp note in that space came from a bottle with a peel."

"Could the catalogue orange trick you," Mabel asked.

"It is louder and lasts," Tessa said. "It leaves its cologne in the air like a boast. Jar 4 does a job and leaves. The cap smelled of something that had already mostly gone."

Mabel nodded once. "Write that. Not the poetry. The part about loud and last."

Tessa wrote, catalogue orange lingers and perfumes. CB12 quick, dull, leaves. Hall cap note brief and sharp, not perfumed.

She took a photograph of the test strips with her phone under raking light and printed it on the little dye-sub she used for restoration records. The image showed what her eyes had found: a clean dull bar, a smeary patch, a glow, a gentle soften. She labelled it and slid it into a sleeve.

"You will give that to Shaw," Mabel said.

"I will," Tessa said. "And I will tell him to keep it for background only. He will let the lab hum the cap and argue with molecules. I will offer him a nose on paper to aim him at the right shelf."

Bramble sighed, which often sounded like agreement. He rose, had a drink from his bowl with the care of a gentleman, then came to sit close because solvents make dogs suspicious and he preferred to supervise.

"Control," Mabel said. "Test your own wax again against clean varnish."

"I will," Tessa said. "If only to keep Len from hating himself more than the job requires."

She took a fresh swab, ran wax across a new square on a second test block, waited, then buffed with an old linen cloth. It bloomed quietly to a soft shine. She pressed a thumb on it and lifted. It took a clean print with no slide. She did the same to Jar 4's square and pressed with the same pressure. Her thumb moved a hair's breadth before stopping. She did not need to measure the distance. She wrote, thumb test: CB12 square gives momentary slip.

Mabel peered under the lamp. "A jury likes that sentence," she said.

"Shaw will prefer numbers," Tessa said. She cut a narrow strip from an offcut of the varnished frame and scuffed the end with fine paper to create a makeshift "cap." She placed the strip on a slope board at a slight incline. A drop from Jar 4 went at the top. It flashed and left a faint dulling. A cotton glove fingertip on that edge slid a shade before biting.

She wrote, incline 5 degrees, glove, CB12 edge catches late.

"Enough," Mabel said. "You are building a yacht. The Inspector asked for an oar."

"He can choose his parts," Tessa said, but she put the bottles away anyway. Jar 4 she recapped tightly and sealed with a band of tape. She wrote the code on the tape and the date. Not evidence, only reference. The others went back on the shelf where they could go on fixing furniture instead of people.

The bell from the front chimed and Constable Hargreaves appeared in the doorway with his standard neatness and a notebook that had seen service. He stayed on the threshold until Tessa waved him past the invisible line that separates shop from back room.

"Inspector said if you started sniffing bottles you'd do it properly," he said. "He asked me to bring you a small box of nothing and then take away a page with everything."

"You get the best jobs," Mabel said.

"Biscuits help," he said.

Tessa handed him the printed photo of the test strips with the labels and her notes on effect and scent. She did not try to hand over any bottle. She pointed at Jar 4's code written in her book. "Tell him that is the brand name and the bite," she said. "Tell him the catalogue orange isn't a match. Tell him Len's wax behaves.

Tell him the test on varnish replicates the dull he will have seen under his light, and that the smell at the cap yesterday was the No. 12 flick, not a kitchen smell."

Hargreaves read the page twice, wrote CB12 quick dull no perfume on his own pad, and slid Tessa's print into a clear wallet.

"He will want the page," he said.

"He may have the page," she said. "But write the words anyway. Phones and printers forget."

He smiled. "We are aligned."

Before he left he sniffed the air out of curiosity and made a face. "It does make the back of the nose sit up," he said. "I do not like it."

"You are not meant to," Mabel said. "It is meant to do a job and leave."

When the room settled again, Tessa opened the small safe and checked the two glassine envelopes. The brass tab with the laurel leaf waited like a coin. The ledger stub with its torn "Phase 1" sat beside it. She added a third sleeve with a copy of the strip photo and a summary. She kept the original notes on her bench, where they belonged.

"Do you believe your own nose," Mabel asked, not doubting, only training the habit of doubt on the right thing.

"I believe it enough to write it down," Tessa said. "I will not call it proof. I will call it direction."

"And the direction," Mabel said.

"Toward Vera's kit," Tessa said. "Not away from her manifest. Toward a brand with a bite and a habit of leaving tidy."

Mabel looked pleased and cross at once. "I do hate a tidy villain," she said. "They keep rooms very clean while they shove people."

"Shaw will lean back toward her when the cap sings," Tessa said. "He is leaning away at the moment because paper makes a noise. Noses make quieter noises. They carry less in court until a lab hums the same tune."

She shut the drawer and washed her hands twice at the little sink. The smell of peel lingered at her sleeves anyway, a ghost note that would follow her to tea if she let it. She changed into the cardigan that lived on the hook for days that required an extra layer between head and world.

They had an hour of peace. People came for frames and tape and a string that was too thin for its ambitions. A child pressed her face to the glass under the hatbox and whispered something to the cup. Bramble approved of all of them impartially.

Near noon, Lin came by with a bag of rosemary cuttings and a verdict on the lavender. "It forgives," he said. "Plants are moral without making speeches."

"Unlike us," Mabel said.

Lin sniffed the room and raised a brow. "Citrus," he said. "That peel again."

"We walked it," Tessa said. "Then put it away."

"Good," Lin said. "Save your noses for bread." He left the rosemary and a list of seed varieties the library should buy and went away cosseting the thought that someone might read it.

Tessa wrote her line for the day in the book because that is what you do when the piece comes to you without fuss.

Tested four. CB12 peels, flashes, dulls clean. Same note at cap. Lemon oil and wax not match. Catalogue orange wrong. Write to Shaw: scent matches kit, effect matches dull patch.

She tucked the page under the counter glass beside the strip photo. The small museum at the corner grew again. Brass laurel. Torn stub. Saucer's start time. Blue chalk. Two clocks disagreeing. Now a printed strip that showed what a bottle could do to shine in a breath.

Mabel poured, set a mug by her elbow, and watched her with that look that never let pride swell too far. "Say the other thing," she said. "The one you do not want to say."

"Someone wiped that cap," Tessa said. "Not in a panic. As part of a tidy. They were thinking about photographs or fingerprints or nothing at all except that they hate smear. They took a wipe that knows varnish and they made a safe place for a hand to fail."

Mabel nodded once. "Write that too," she said. "Then stop for today."

"I will stop," Tessa said.

The bell chimed and Isla's father stood there with a face that had done hard jobs this week. He held a tin under one arm like a person carrying a bird that might fly. He placed it on the counter and opened it with care. Inside sat a Victoria sponge, patient and steady.

"From the house," he said. "For helping. For the dog. For the Inspector if you need an excuse to get him here."

"We never need an excuse," Mabel said. "But we will pretend we did."

He smiled with a crooked kindness and left.

Tessa cut a small wedge and made herself taste it without thinking of anything she could not change. She let the sugar do the ordinary thing sugar does when it is not being asked to lend opinions to timelines. Then she wrote one more spare line beneath the solvent notes.

Hall cap and CB12 speak the same way. Lab to confirm. Do not get ahead of it.

She shut the book and put the pen down. Outside the yard, a blackbird argued with its reflection in the window and then decided it had better things to do. Inside, the bench smelled of cotton and the very faint end of peel. Bramble snored. The day held to its work.

THIRTEEN

Sunday afternoon laid a soft lid on Fernvale. After the morning's alibi dance, the village wanted quiet jobs, not noise. Tessa wiped the repair bench, checked the safe, and set the small museum of evidence under the counter glass straight. Brass laurel tab. Torn ledger stub with Phase 1 peeking. Dot's photo of the saucer on the Locke box at 9:12. The blue chalk strip and the two-clock print from the garage. The solvent strip. Threads waiting for a needle.

Mabel arrived with a packet of custard creams and a sentence that solved nothing but sounded helpful. "We should walk," she said. "And look at things that do not expect us."

"Notice board," Tessa said. "Then Martin. I want to test my

memory against wood and paper."

Bramble sprang up when he heard the lead, then sat like a saint while Tessa clipped him in. The three of them took Ivy Lane at a pace that made sense for thought.

Fernvale Hall had shed its police tape but not its attention. People kept their voices down on the path as if loud words might stir the stairs. Inside, the foyer smelled of carnations and copied notices. The community board held its usual mosaic of life. Yoga, bell ringing, the autumn gala rota with high-vis vests drawn in biro, a poster with The Laurel Trust printed in green, and a scatter of photographs mounted on card with corners that pretended to be tasteful.

Tessa stood an arm's length away and let her eyes catalogue. Spring Fete prizes, including the tin teapot keyrings she had clocked before. A volunteer day with the Canal Gate wide open and Martin pointing at a bollard as if it were a donor. A group shot from July's fire drill, everyone laughing because the alarms had refused to cooperate. And there, half covered by a flyer for toddler rhyme time, a candid from the summer concert rehearsal. Len at the hook board in his office doorway, holding up two keys with novelty fobs so the choir would remember which hook to use. One teapot and one spoon. The teapot caught the light on its lid, a little nick on the edge where tin shows tin.

Tessa raised her phone, took a photograph at a slight angle to avoid her reflection, then pointed. "That nick," she said.

Mabel leaned in without smudging the glass. "Same family as the dust outline upstairs," she said. "Lid and belly."

"Same as the raffle prize," Tessa said. "They bought a batch. They put hats on keys and prizes on tables. It means nothing and something at the same time."

They moved down one photo. August committee picnic on the green. A table with a paper cloth, the sponsorship board leaning against a chair. Martin's hand in the frame, his face turned away, a key ring on the table beside his cup. Teapot again. The lens had caught the curve of the spout and that tiny nick on the lid. No label, no helpful caption, only habit caught by chance.

"Helpful enough," Mabel said.

They crossed the foyer to Len's office. He looked up when he saw them and then looked past them to the board in the hall as if his keys had gone walking again. "He has them," he said, meaning Shaw. "He will tell me what I should have done in the tense that forgives nothing."

"We came to ask for a different book," Tessa said. "Not your ledger. Your old key register. The one you hate."

Len grimaced, then reached into the bottom drawer and pulled out a blue binder that had once been proud. He opened it on the desk and the dust at the hinge made a small cloud. Columns ruled and ignored. Names scrawled and then forgotten. The last section had cleaner entries, a sign that despair sometimes gives way to resolve.

"Show me Spare B," Tessa said.

He turned to August. Someone had tried headings on that page. Hook label. Key ID. Fob. Holder. Date out. Date in. Notes. The neatness of an intention that had not spread as far as it should. Len's writing looked tired but careful.

"There," he said, tapping with a chewed pencil. "Spare B. Fob: tin teapot. July twelfth, duplicate cut, ref 2B. Issued to choir leader for Thursday practice, returned. July nineteenth, issued to Fernvale Players, returned with biscuit tied to ring, because of course. August second, issued to Trust, M. Hale, Canal Gate and back corridor tour. Return logged. August sixteenth, loaned for Harvest Fair prep, no signature because I was shouted at by twelve women holding glue guns. No return logged. I wrote missing on the eighteenth. I put a circle round it because circles make things behave."

He had indeed written missing in block letters beside Spare B, then circled it as if that might summon the key back through a wall. Beneath Spare B sat a new line in pencil. Spare B, duplicate,

2B, teapot. Issued August twenty third, Laurel Trust office, Sian, key chest swap. Returned ticked, then unticked, then ticked again in a different pen.

"You made a second copy," Tessa said.

"After the first walked," Len said. "It is my curse. Make a duplicate and it grows legs."

"Two teapot fobs then," Mabel said. "One missing since last month. One in circulation."

Len nodded, miserable. "Mrs Dray bought bags of the silly things for the fete. We put them on rings to help people notice a hook. People noticed and then forgot."

"Who has the duplicate today," Tessa asked.

"It should be on the hook," Len said. "It is not. I have been pretending to myself that someone put it in a pocket and meant to hang it back at lunch."

Tessa looked up at the board. Spare B sat bare. The clean arc behind the screw had a fresher brightness than the old teapot halo above it. A second shadow had been there, shorter, recently, then gone. She remembered Hargreaves pointing it out yesterday, the twin arc that told a story in dust.

"You cut the duplicate where," she asked.

"Cargill's," Len said. "He hates novelty tops. He only cuts the blade. I added the stupid hat after."

"You keep the invoice," Mabel said.

Len went into a different drawer, the one that held Bills That Argue. He produced a slip dated 23 August. Duplicate key cut, SB-2. Price written with the thrift of a man who wants fewer copies made. He had written teapot on the receipt because it mattered to him which hat lived on which blade.

Tessa took a photograph of the page and the invoice and wrote the dates on her pad. July twelfth, duplicate cut, Spare B. August eighteenth, Spare B logged missing. August twenty third, second duplicate cut, Spare B-2. She added, Martin issued August second

145

for Canal Gate tour, returned. Sian issued August twenty third, returned on paper then unticked then ticked. She did not like the dance of the ticks.

"May I photograph the missing circle," she asked.

"Take the book if you want," Len said. "It is the only way it will learn its lesson."

"I do not need the object," Tessa said. "I need the lines." She took one more photo to catch a detail at the bottom of the page. Someone had written in a tidy, unfamiliar hand, Duplicate key rings to be relabelled with neutral fobs. That was Martin's voice in someone else's pen. She filed it without a label she would regret.

They left Len to his penance and crossed the foyer again. Tessa lifted the edge of the toddler flyer on the photo with the teapot and took a second shot, sharp and closer. Then she stood in front of the poster for the gala and read the sponsor tiers against her better judgment. Silver leaf, gold leaf, laurel. She did not smile.

"Martin," Mabel said mildly, as if summoning a kettle.

They walked the short path to the malt house. Sian waved them through with the look of a woman who had been given three lists and one pair of hands. Martin's door was open. He sat at his desk with his jacket off and a spreadsheet that refused to love him.

"Ladies," he said, easy. "I was about to pretend I am done for the day. You will save me from pretending."

Tessa did not sit. Her eyes went to the right corner of his desk where a tray held his daily detritus. A pen, a phone, a paper knife in the shape of a gull, a key ring. Tin teapot. The same lid nick caught the light through the sash window. She looked, not long enough to be rude, long enough to be exact. The blade below the fob had a tiny number scratched by a nail on the shoulder. 2B. Cargill's habit when a customer insists on a mark and he is out of tags.

"Busy," Martin said, following her glance with the reflex of a man who always knows what sits on his furniture. "Can I pretend you are here to bring me cake."

"We are here to bring you a question," Tessa said. "Spare B."

He smiled in the way people do when they decide you are making weather out of mist. "The volunteer's curse," he said. "It goes walking and returns with a story." He picked up the ring and let the teapot swing. "You admire the hat."

"I admire the nick," Tessa said. "Left lid. I saw it on the notice board in July, in a photo with Len holding up hooks. I saw it again on the green at the picnic, next to your cup. I see it here."

"The village bought dozens," he said. "I wear one because Mrs Dray will take away my biscuits if I do not. It may be the same one in every photograph. It may be a cousin. You would need a blacksmith to tell you."

"We have Len's register," Tessa said. "Spare B duplicate cut on the twenty third last month. Blade marked 2B. Issued to Sian for the key chest swap, then the ticks had an argument. One Spare B logged missing on the eighteenth. That is the other. Two teapot rings, one missing. This on your desk carries 2B scratched into the shoulder."

Martin turned the key to the light, squinted, and laughed once. "Cargill always leaves his hieroglyphs," he said. "I borrowed this on Friday for a supplier route and then forgot to put it back because I am undisciplined. I will take my scolding like a man."

"Borrowed," Mabel said. "From whom."

"From the hook," he said. "Len's board. He was out the back with a mop and an opinion. I signed nothing because I am a hypocrite who likes to tell people to sign things. I intended to return it after my walk round Canal Gate."

"Which you did not," Tessa said.

"Which I did not," he said. "I left it on the desk under a brochure because the phone rang. It has not opened any doors that did not belong to me. You may take a photograph with your disapproval."

She did not. She only looked at the number again and watched the way his hand rested on the ring. Casual. Habit. Ownership is a mood more than a fact.

"Your July duplicate," she said. "Why did you cut it."

"I did not cut anything," he said. "I asked Len to solve a nuisance. The choir had a system, the drama group had another, Spare B came back in pockets with lipstick on the ring. Len sighed and went to Cargill with a scrap of money and a prayer. I signed off in theory. He did the work."

"And the first Spare B," Tessa said. "The one logged missing on the eighteenth."

Martin's expression did not change. He had the self-possession of a person who has practised his face in mirrors meant for donors. "If you think I have it in my desk," he said, almost amused, "you are welcome to open every drawer."

"I think you have the duplicate on your desk," Tessa said. "And I think the first walked in August and grew a story. Who told it to go I cannot yet say."

He set the ring down and folded his hands. "If you discover my secretary has been sabotaging doors with novelty hats, I will take my punishment in cake," he said. "Until then, I suggest you speak to Cargill. He knows which blade belongs to which week better than any of us."

"We will," Tessa said.

She let her gaze drift to the credenza. The sponsorship board lay there still, the line he had edited to match the foyer poster visible through the tissue. A small brass tray beside it held clips and tabs for plaques. Among them, Tessa saw one of the little brass leaves with a tiny hole punched for a ring, a twin to the tab Bramble had nosed from the spool. She said nothing. The tray was not a crime. It was a habit of tidiness in a room that wrote grants for a living.

Sian knocked and put her head in with that efficient kindness that keeps offices from collapsing. "Mr Hale, the trustee with strong feelings is on two," she said. "He has found a synonym for cohesion and wants to share."

"Save me," Martin said, then to Tessa, "If you require the key, take it and hang it back for Len. He will forgive you. He likes you."

"We require a photograph," Tessa said. She took a close shot of the blade shoulder with the 2B scratch, then a wider one of the teapot fob with its nick. "Thank you."

"Thank you," he echoed, already reaching for the phone. "Ms Harper, you may not like some of my methods, but I do not break locks to keep a hall in funds."

"I prefer not to like anyone's methods," she said, and stepped out.

Back at the hall, they found Len with his pencil and patience. Tessa showed him the photograph of the 2B scratch and the notice-board images. He breathed out in a way that sounded like consent to gravity.

"That is the duplicate," he said. "I put 2B on the shoulder with Cargill's nail because I promised myself I would not lose it like the first. I lost it anyway to a man with a printer and a conscience. He will bring it back in an envelope and pretend it was a system."

"Missing Spare B," Mabel said. "Tell us who took it last."

Len checked the register again as if the answer might have changed since lunch. "No signature," he said. "My fault. It was the week of the harvest prep. Everyone borrowed everything. The last time I remember seeing the teapot hat was at the Friday rehearsal for the play. Vera was there to fix a bow. Poppy had a ribbon on her wrist like a bracelet. Delia flapped. Martin stopped me in the corridor to say the Gate would need a steward at both ends. Then I saw the teapot ring on the back corridor hook and felt better. After that everything tasted like haste."

"Shaw will ask Cargill to check his book," Tessa said. "But we have enough to write on paper. Two teapot fobs. Spare B logged missing eighteen August. Duplicate, 2B, on Martin's desk today."

Len nodded and rubbed the bridge of his nose. "I will buy a label maker and live a quieter life," he said.

They found Shaw at The Thimble & Fern where his pencil had made a small fort again. He listened, wrote Spare B missing 18 Aug, 2B on Hale desk, photographed July photo of nicked fob, wrote Cargill invoice 23 Aug, and did not ask for more colour than that.

"This helps," he said. "Keys are more honest than people, until they go missing. You have given me two hats and two dates. I will go and bother a locksmith until he remembers cutting 2B and then I will ask him whether anyone asked for novelty blanks. Then I will ask Mr Hale why his hand sits so naturally on a key ring that should not live on his desk on a Sunday."

"He will tell you he borrowed," Mabel said.

"I expect he will," Shaw said. "He will also tell me whether he borrowed on Friday night as well as Saturday morning. The back corridor door log shows the reader registered two rings between seven and eight. One of them was Len. The other was a cousin."

"A cousin," Tessa said. "Back corridor has no electronics."

"The back corridor has a mechanical sensor we forgot," Shaw said, pleased. "The door tradesmen use. It tells me when the bolt moves. It tells me only time, not blade. It sang twice Friday evening. Len's handwriting gives me one. The other line will belong to a hand that will not enjoy hearing me say the time."

"Seven thirty five," Tessa said.

"Seven thirty five," he echoed, amused. "Mr Hale began his speech about fire exits at seven thirty eight. He could have done it from the corridor if he wished."

He closed the notebook. "Thank you," he said. "You have given me a thread. Watch now as I pull it and hope it does not take the roof."

Back at Ink & Ivy, the kettle behaved, which felt like a small rebate on a week that had not offered many. Tessa slid the new photographs under the glass. The teapot lid nick now sat beside the blue chalk line and the strip of dulling varnish like three small voices that, together, began to sound like a statement.

Mabel ate a biscuit the way a woman does when she does not intend to apologise for liking sugar. "You think Martin has the taste for shoving," she said.

"I think Martin has the taste for control," Tessa said. "The shove might belong to someone else. The key shows he could find a quiet moment on a door that ought to have resisted him if he had turned up with only his virtue. That is all it says today. It says he is at the table."

"And the missing Spare B," Mabel said.

"Walked a month ago and did not return," Tessa said. "It could still surface in a pocket, looking foolish. Or it could live in a glovebox and think itself useful."

Bramble thumped his tail at that because glovebox meant car and car meant walks. Tessa obliged by ruffling his ears. He had done as much as any living soul to earn a biscuit in this case. He received one with dignity.

At four, Sian came in with her neat fringe and a folder, her mouth set in a line that said she had decided to stop apologising for other people's charms. She set the folder on the counter.

"Mr Hale asked me to return this to Len," she said, and slid out the ring with 2B. "He forgot he had it. He asked me to say that as if it would help. I will take the scolding now."

"You will take tea," Mabel said. "We do not scold messengers."

Sian softened by two degrees. "Thank you," she said. "Also, the locksmith rang. He left a message to say the man with strong opinions has already been. He says he will sleep fine without novelty blanks in his shop."

"Good," Tessa said. "We will all sleep better when keys learn how to come home without drama."

After she left, Tessa wrote three lines in her book with the simple pleasure of a fact that does not hide.

Notice board shows teapot fob with lid nick in July and August photos. Len's register: Spare B logged missing 18 Aug; second Spare B cut 23 Aug, blade marked 2B. 2B seen on Martin's desk, returned by Sian at 16:04.

She added, smaller, back corridor sensor showed two opens Fri 19:32 window, second not Len. Then she slid the page under the glass and stood back to look at the corner museum. It had begun to look less like a jumble and more like a model. Not solved. Only set.

Mabel rested her chin on her hand and watched the kettle do its trick. "We are getting close to the room," she said.

"We are standing in the door," Tessa said. "We can smell the varnish and see the light. Now we have to count the feet."

She poured and let the steam do the civilising work it has done in this country longer than anyone can remember. Outside, the canal held its temper. Inside, the dog slept and the teapot fob glinted once under the counter glass as if trying to join a conversation. It had, in its little way. That would have to do for today.

FOURTEEN

Len telephoned at noon and asked Tessa to come to the hall without fuss. His voice sounded older by a decade. She took Mabel and Bramble because some rooms go easier with witnesses and a dog.

He met them in the foyer, cap in hand. His eyes had the look of a man who had decided to put himself in order before anyone else did.

"In here," he said, and led them into the office behind the door.

Papers lay in three neat piles on the desk. The bucket lived in the corner, clean and sulking. Len shut the door with care and sat, not at the chair behind the desk, at the visitor chair, as if to put himself on the wrong side of the counter.

"I will say it plain," he began. "I double-booked for cash. I took small fees from people who wanted the side room when the main hall had a rehearsal. I told myself it kept the place alive. I polished my own floors on off days and I took a fiver to do it faster when I should have taken none. I moved the sign to suit photographs. I am not a killer," he added, steady. "I am a bad bookkeeper with pride."

Mabel folded her hands. "Thank you," she said. "Plain saves time."

Len nodded once, grateful. "Inspector Shaw will have it all in a minute. I wanted you to hear it first so you do not waste any art on me."

"We prefer facts to art," Tessa said.

He pulled a clipboard from the hook and set it on the desk, then slid across a slim blue folder. "Outage sheet," he said, patting the board. "Door sign-in list for this week," he said, tapping the folder. "I have not altered a line since Friday. I have not filled any gaps since you asked for the first glance. I am tired of being the sort of man who writes later."

Tessa stood to read without touching. The outage sheet on the board was the same grid she had seen in his hands before, with Friday's dimmer run and mains test. Now, on Saturday's blank line, a new small block had been added at the bottom margin in tidy print, boxed off with a ruler. Vendor window, anteroom, 09:58–10:06. Beneath it, the name: V. Locke. The letters sat exact, upright, no loops, no flourish. It was not Len's round hand. It was not Delia's lilt. It matched the labels on Vera's bottles to the stroke.

"Who wrote this block," Tessa asked.

"I did not," Len said at once. "She did, with my pen, while we were talking about the banner drop. She said I would thank her later for tidy paperwork. I was glad someone else liked boxes." He rubbed his eyebrow. "I liked it until yesterday, when boxes started looking like traps."

Tessa kept her face still. "When did she add it."

"After ten," he said. "But she wrote 09:58 because she said it reads cleaner to start before. She laughed when she said it. I did not like the laugh. I did not dislike it either. I was in flight by then, if you know what I mean. I wanted the morning to stop moving."

"Did you initial it," Mabel asked.

He shook his head. "I would have if she had left the board on the hook. She wrote, she boxed it, she set the board down to one side, then we all ran off to look at flowers and swags. I did not look again. When the day went wrong, I went nowhere near paper."

"Inspector Shaw will want this exact sentence," Tessa said. "He will want the board as it sits, and the time you say she touched it."

Len put both palms on his knees like a man bracing against a wave. "He can have my knees as well."

"Let us look at the sign-in list," Mabel said.

Len opened the blue folder and turned to the current week. The pages were ruled into columns: day, door, time in, time out, name, initials. The lines showed the truth of a village week. Choir, florist, decorator, Locke & Linen driver, electrician, volunteers. Friday had a block of entries between seven and eight. Len's own hand, then a second hand. The second hand did not belong to him. It did not belong to Delia. It belonged to a person who made straight stems and flat caps, who wrote in tidy small capitals and used even pressure. VERA LOCKE, it said for 19:34, anteroom, time out blank. On Saturday the same hand appeared at 09:59 with an out at 10:06. Both blocks had the name printed in full, not a scrawl. Both had the same squared E and the same narrow R.

"Why is Friday's time out blank," Tessa asked.

"Habit," Len said. "She floats, then she flies. Vendors do. They do not bring their pens back to kiss the line. I meant to fill it with her name later. I did not."

"Why is Saturday's so neat," Mabel asked. "No one writes that square when they are working."

"She wrote it," Len said. "She said she would save me five minutes. She set it in a box of her own and told me to file it later."

Tessa leaned in until the paper filled her field of view. The Saturday block had a faint dent at the top left corner where a ruler had pressed. The Friday block did not. Ink tone matched Saturday's new box on the outage sheet. The strokes were firmer than Len's pencil. The neat, clinical E, three equal bars, had caught her eye in Vera's warehouse on the bottles. She remembered the label on Citrus Remover No. 12 where someone had written NO. 12 in that same square style. She did not feel triumph. She felt the click a drawer makes when it closes.

"Door," Mabel said, reading the Friday line. "Back corridor."

Len nodded, mortified. "I know what you are about to say. The sensor sang twice. One was me at nineteen thirty two. One was someone with a cousin key at nineteen thirty five or thereabouts. I did not hear the second because Delia was telling me to admire the fade."

"You are not the only person in this building who missed things," Mabel said kindly.

Len passed a hand over his face. "I have kept my sins to myself for years," he said. "Double bookings, a tenner for an extra hour, the odd off-list hire when the parish needed a place on a wet day. The Trustees do not love cash. The parish does. I thought I was helping. I like floors. I like their shine. I like lists. I thought lists would make me safe."

"Lists make liars safe only for a while," Tessa said. "Then the lines begin to say other things."

He pointed at the outage sheet on the board. "The mains test on Friday has my initials," he said. "The dimmer run has mine. The note that says Fade to candle trial per DP was written in Delia's hand the day before, when we printed the sheet. The Saturday vendor box sits where it does because Vera wrote it on Saturday and I did not stop her. She wrote her name in my book because she writes her name on everything in her sight. If you tell me this makes me an accessory to murder I will walk to the station without my coat."

"It makes you a man who let a neat person make a neat habit," Mabel said. "The Inspector will still point at your pride. You can bear it. You are old enough."

A knock sounded. Constable Hargreaves stood in the doorway with a polite face and a bag for paper. Shaw had sent him to fetch the same things Len had set out.

"Mr Porter," Hargreaves said. "Inspector requests your outage board and your sign-in sheets. He asks that you do not tidy for him."

"I have already confessed to a stranger on a bus," Len said. "Take my sins and my paper."

Hargreaves took the board, slid it into a rigid sleeve, then lifted the blue folder with both hands. He did not look at the pages. He had the air of a man ferrying bread. He nodded to Tessa. "Anything you want me to tell him with the paper."

"Tell him the Saturday vendor block and the Friday anteroom entry sit in Vera Locke's tidy print," Tessa said. "Tell him the Saturday box was added after ten with a ruler and Len's pen. Tell him Friday's out box is blank."

Hargreaves wrote that on his pad in his own neatness and tucked it in with the board. "He will like the ruler," he said.

When he had gone, Len sagged a fraction, then straightened. He reached for the bucket and then left it where it was. The act felt like growth.

"I did polish on Thursday night," he said, as if he had found one more piece of honesty to hand over. "Not where the landing sits. The side hall. I tell you because you will smell wax there and I do not want to watch you write poetry when it is only me being me. The main landing I hit first thing Saturday because I wanted the shine for the photographer. I used my blend. No lemon. No citrus. My fault remains plain. I made a runway. Another hand did the pushing."

Tessa nodded. "We saw the runway," she said. "We saw where the run starts. We smelled the cap. Your wax and your pride helped someone. They did not shove."

Len stared at the floor as if it had betrayed him. "I will take my scolding with grace," he said. "I will repaint the back door and shine shoes in the porch until Christmas. I will make amends with work. I was built for work."

Mabel touched his sleeve. "You will also sleep," she said. "Shaw will not break you for being foolish in a village. He will breathe on you. That is his style."

Len almost smiled. "He breathes like a baritone," he said. "I will bring biscuits to his table and ask him to aim at men who deserve it."

They left him to his lists and walked back into the airy foyer. The notice board glared with seasonal cheer. The photo of Len holding the two novelty fobs now felt less cute and more like a telegram. Outside, the day had turned honest. Clouds cleared to a simple blue. The canal moved as if schedules meant nothing to water.

At The Thimble & Fern, Shaw sat where he sat when paper was coming his way, pencil ready, cup ignored. Hargreaves arrived a minute after them and set the board and the folder down like trophies.

"Report," Shaw said.

Hargreaves relayed Tessa's sentence about the Saturday vendor block, the ruler dent, the neat print, the Friday blank, the time Len remembered for the addition.

Shaw lifted the board and looked at the Saturday box. He did not touch the ink. He read the letters as if they were a familiar label on a bottle. Then he set the board down and opened the blue folder at Friday. He covered various columns with one hand as he read, a habit of his, to make columns speak in turn. He stopped with his finger on the 19:34 anteroom entry. He did not need anyone to tell him whose print he was reading.

"Good," he said. "This is ugly in the helpful way. Ms Locke writes herself clean and late. Mr Porter confesses to being the sort of man who charges five pounds to keep a choir dry. One of these sins sits in court. The other reminds a vicar to use volunteers."

He flicked to Saturday and looked at 09:59 to 10:06, then at the vendor box on the outage sheet again. He wrote the two times on a slip of paper and slid it into his pocket where he kept minutes he liked.

"Any other names added late," he asked Hargreaves.

"None with that hand," Hargreaves said. "Most entries live in Len's pencil or a florist's flourish."

Shaw shut the folder. "Bring me Ms Locke and Mr Hale in the morning," he said. "Not together. Mr Porter will give me his pride in a statement, then he will go home and polish only furniture he owns. I will talk to the electrician about that back corridor sensor again. It enjoys being right."

He turned to Tessa. "Thank you," he said. "You can tell when a hand sits on the wrong page."

"It sits too straight," Tessa said. "It loves itself more than the column does."

He allowed a brief smile. "Poetic," he said. "Do not do that in front of the jury."

Mabel put a plate of jam tarts between them and became Switzerland. "Eat," she said. "You are both thin as rules."

Shaw obeyed, which meant he took two and pretended it was duty.

Back at Ink & Ivy, Tessa set her notebook on the counter and wrote three clean lines.

Len confessed double bookings, cash, and his own polish on Thursday and Saturday. Outage sheet now shows a Saturday vendor box, 09:58–10:06, added late in Vera's tidy print. Door sign-in list carries Friday 19:34 anteroom entry in the same hand, time out blank.

She added, smaller, ruler dent at Saturday box, ink tone matches, same squared E. Then she slid the page under the glass among the other small truths. The little museum grew again, not crowded, only ready.

Mabel watched her with that old fondness mixed with rigour. "You feel the net tighten," she said.

"I feel the timing learn to speak," Tessa said. "We can hear who likes paper, who likes polish, who likes power."

"Write that down and then stop," Mabel said. "We will need our energy tomorrow."

Tessa wrote one last line.

Neat print arrives after the fact. Pride arrives before. The push borrows both.

FIFTEEN

By late afternoon the village had settled into its Sunday quiet. The Thimble & Fern kept the sort of hum that lets talk sit level. Shaw had his corner again, pencil squared with the edge of the table, cup going cold because he used tea the way other men use paperweights.

Tessa sat opposite with her notebook open to a fresh page. Mabel brought two shortbreads and declared them neutral. Bramble sprawled under the table and took his duties seriously, which today meant sleeping with intent.

"Let us turn fog into minutes," Shaw said. "Cleanly."

"Fog likes minutes," Mabel said. "They give it edges."

Shaw opened a slim evidence envelope and slid out a photocopy of the outage sheet, a single-page print from a door sensor log, and two small piles of phone records. One carried Laurel Trust letterhead. The other wore Locke & Linen branding and the resigned look of data that knows it will be blamed.

"Outage first," he said, tapping the sheet. "Friday. Skylight dimmer fade, nineteen thirty two to thirty nine. Mains test, nineteen forty one to forty two."

He wrote the times on the table napkin in a neat line. 19:32–19:39, fade. 19:41–19:42, mains. His pencil left small tidy marks that always made Tessa like him more than she meant to.

"Door sensor," he said, the small satisfaction of a man who loves a machine that tells the truth. "Back corridor tradesmen's bolt logged two movements during the fade run. Nineteen thirty two and nineteen thirty five. The first is Mr Porter. He admits it and writes like a man who respects hinges. The second belongs to a cousin key."

"Spare B's cousin," Tessa said.

"Spare B's cousin," he echoed. "The mechanical sensor gives time to the second because the man who installed it liked to boast. Nineteen thirty two and eleven seconds. Nineteen thirty five and fifty four."

He wrote 19:32:11, 19:35:54 below the dimmer line.

"Phone logs," he said, and slid the Laurel Trust print across to Tessa. Martin's calls for Friday sat in a calm column. The one that mattered wore a small star in Sian's neat hand. Incoming, 19:35, from H. Carline, duration 00:05:38, answered. End 19:41:03.

"Carline," Mabel said. "The councillor who uses cohesion like butter."

"The same," Shaw said. "Mr Hale stepped out of the rehearsal at nineteen thirty five to take that call in the corridor because he likes to be seen being useful. The call ended at nineteen forty one. He went back in as the mains test began."

He turned to Vera's page. Her company report for Friday showed calls at 18:59, then nothing again until 20:07. No call activity at all in the dimmer window. He set that sheet aside.

"Receipt clock," he said, warming to the tidy, "to keep us honest. The Thimble & Fern's till prints seconds. I asked for Friday's tape. It shows a takeaway tea for Mr Hale at nineteen forty eight and thirty two. Paid on card. He came here after the rehearsal and ordered with the face men use when they want to be seen having a community."

Mabel held up the roll by its edge, proud. "Our clock does not drift," she said. "It syncs to a little black box the brewer insists on. It is correct to the second. We have checked it against his phone within a heartbeat."

Shaw wrote 19:48:32 tea, Hale in his tidy line and set the pencil down a moment. The napkin had become a small road.

Tessa looked at the four pieces and felt them settle. Fade from 19:32 to 19:39. Bolt at 19:32:11. Bolt again at 19:35:54. Hale's call begins 19:35:26, ends 19:41:03. Mains cut 19:41 to 19:42. Tea bought 19:48:32 by a man who had decided he had done enough for one evening.

"Who is in the landing at nineteen thirty four," she asked, not for poetry. For the answer that would hold shape.

"Not Len," Shaw said. "He is in the hall with a torch and a hymn about fire exits. Not Hale. He is in the corridor on his phone. Not Isla, not Poppy. They are in the main room rearranging chairs and touching ribbon they are not allowed to touch. Not the photographer, who stood at the end of the aisle pretending the candle trial mattered. The person who wrote her name in neat print on the anteroom line at nineteen thirty four has business near that landing. Ms Locke."

He pulled the blue folder he had taken from Len earlier and opened the sign-in sheet for Friday. The line sat there in Vera's square hand: 19:34, anteroom. Time out box blank. It looked like neatness and care. It looked like something else when put beside a door bolt and a dimmer.

"She had the corridor between nineteen thirty four and nineteen forty," Tessa said. "At least six minutes without Hale, with light lowering and hands reaching for the rail. She signs in, he takes a call, the bolt moves again at nineteen thirty five fifty four. If she wanted to adjust a bow at the doorway, she would be on that landing in the darkest minute. If she wanted to test a wipe in grey, same."

"Six minutes," Shaw said. "If we take the second bolt at face value, five minutes and nine seconds between nineteen thirty five and the mains test. If we give her the minute before Hale's call, a shade over six."

He wrote the bracket on the napkin. [19:34–19:40]. Then he underlined it once, the way he did with things he meant to keep.

"Alone," he said. "Because the person who would stand beside her to talk to donors stepped away to charm a councillor."

Mabel tapped the sign-in sheet with one clean nail. "The tidy print matters," she said. "If a person writes themselves into a box, they are there to be seen. If no one looks, the box does the looking for them later."

"Why put her name in at all," Tessa asked. "If she wanted fog, no paper would be better."

"Because she loves order," Shaw said. "Because she believes herself safe. Because writing your name in a place you think is yours feels like staking a claim."

He had the look of a man whose map had just given him a road he did not have to build. He turned the door log around so they could all read the small numbers without squinting. He placed the outage sheet beside it so the brackets sat on the same line.

"Saturday morning," he said. "The vendor box, nine fifty eight to ten oh six, written in the same tidy hand. She makes herself a window. It lives on paper. You showed me it was added late. You showed me Friday's line is hers too. The pattern repeats. Rehearsal, then performance."

Mabel brought more tea with the air of someone who knew when to push sugar and when to keep quiet. Bramble chose that moment to turn over with a sigh that sounded like agreement. Tessa watched Shaw let the seconds arrange themselves into a thing he could carry into a room full of people with opinions.

"We need one more anchor," Tessa said, always careful with the way pride can make a person jump a rung. "The mains test began at nineteen forty one. Hale's call ended at nineteen forty one oh three. If he left the corridor at once and came up toward the landing, he would reach it within twenty seconds. She had him gone for the whole run. She had the full six."

Shaw nodded, already writing. "I will ask Mr Hale to do what men like him hate," he said. "Walk it. From his office door to the landing at his usual pace. I will time his shoes. If they say nineteen forty one and thirty one, I will smile privately. If they say nineteen forty two, I will smile publicly."

He folded the napkin and tucked it into his pocket with care, as if a paper with graphite could be a tool. He returned to the phone logs and tapped Vera's page.

"She does not call in the window," he said. "She does not receive. Her phone sits quiet. That is not proof. It keeps me from being distracted by an alibi that is louder than it is useful."

He turned to a second receipt roll from the café. "While I was in a generous mood, I also asked for Saturday's tape," he said. "Because Ms Harper likes receipts. We have Delia buying two coffees at ten twelve and forty seven. We have Vera buying nothing. We have Mr Hale buying a bottle of water at ten twenty eight before going back to the hall because he is a man who thinks hydration is diligence."

Tessa wrote the times out of habit. It soothed her to see the shapes in ink. She added, smaller, café clock correct to seconds. She added a line that had become a retrain this week: do not marry a receipt, but you can like it.

Shaw sat back. He drummed his pencil once, then stopped himself because he disliked the sound. "I leaned away from Vera this morning," he said. "Her manifest and her fuel slip have weight. Your dashcam cloud took some from the slip. This gives me back more. Six minutes alone on the landing during a scheduled dim, with Mr Hale actively elsewhere. That is not a whisper, it is a sentence."

"Paper gives it to you," Mabel said. "You like paper."

"I do," he said. "Even when it scolds me."

He rose. "I am going to the hall to make Mr Hale walk his corridor with me," he said. "Then I will ask Ms Locke about her habit of writing boxes after ten o'clock on a Saturday morning and at nineteen thirty four on a Friday evening. I will ask her where she stood at nineteen thirty seven. I will ask what she touched."

He left the café with the napkin in his pocket. The room exhaled around his absence. People resumed their gossip about the price of eggs and the parish raffle as if this small choreography of seconds had not just altered the week.

Mabel looked at Tessa. "You are thinking about the cap again," she said.

"I am thinking that in grey people steady themselves with their palms," Tessa said. "And that Jar Four left a clean dull that makes a hand slide before it grips. If she tested it on Friday, she learned the feel. If she tested, she will have told herself she was fixing a smear for the camera."

"People tell themselves comforting things before they shove," Mabel said. "It is human."

They walked to the hall, because some things are best seen, not recited. The foyer had its usual tired cheer. The landing looked like a landing again and not a theatre. Len appeared at the office door with his pen like a flag of truce.

"Inspector said you might come," he said. "He asked me not to polish until Christmas."

"That suits us all," Mabel said.

Shaw arrived with Mr Hale two minutes later, the two of them in step in the way men are when one of them is leading and both pretend not to notice.

"Evening rehearsal," Shaw said to Hale, without preamble. "You took a call at nineteen thirty five, here." He stood at the office threshold. "You ended the call at nineteen forty one and three seconds. Walk with me to the landing at your usual pace, please. No theatre."

They walked. Shaw did not hurry him. He did not dawdle him either. He held his phone at chest height where it would read seconds without fuss. They reached the landing turn, the place where the cap sits a shade duller than its neighbours, at nineteen forty one and thirty five by the phone. Hale rested his hand on the cap without thinking, then snatched it away because he is a man who does not like to be caught being human.

"Thirty five," Shaw said, showing him the screen. "If you ended a call at nineteen forty one and three seconds, you would arrive here at thirty five. Ms Locke signed into the anteroom at nineteen thirty four. The dimmer run ended at nineteen thirty nine. The mains went off at nineteen forty one. The cap did not help anyone between thirty four and forty."

Hale's face did not acquire guilt. It acquired calculation. "You are telling me a vendor had a window," he said, taking refuge in his language.

"I am telling you she had six minutes," Shaw said. "And I am telling you that at least one of those minutes was as dark as you thought poetry should be."

Hale did not flinch. He picked up his phone, looked at a screen that already knew what it had done on Friday evening, and then put it down again. "You have paper," he said. "You will have my apology for the key on my desk. You will have my scolding for Mr Porter in written form, because I know how to write those. You will not have a speech from me about how much I dislike this conclusion."

"I would dislike it too if I had pressed for cohesion at the speed of minutes," Shaw said. "We are not here for speeches."

He turned to Tessa and nodded once, the thank you of a man who has been given a bolt that fits his door. She did not smile. She had no room for that. She was too busy counting the steps from an office to a cap.

In the evening, back at Ink & Ivy, the small museum under the counter glass gained a new scrap: a copy of the napkin, rewritten on paper with straight lines and the times in her own hand. 19:32–19:39 fade. 19:35:26–19:41:03 Hale call. 19:32:11 and 19:35:54 bolts. 19:34 anteroom, V. Locke, out blank. Window for Vera: six minutes minimum. She tucked it in beside the solvent strip and the blue chalk line.

Mabel poured tea and pushed a plate of shortbread into the middle because sometimes the only answer to minutes is sugar. Bramble snored, then woke as if to give his opinion, which he did by standing, turning twice, and settling again.

"Say it," Mabel said. "Say what you will not put in your statement."

"Friday was the rehearsal," Tessa said. "Saturday was the performance. She tested the wipe in grey. She learned how the cap feels when it stops being a friend. She wrote herself a Saturday box because paper makes her feel clean. Then she took a window in glare and pretended it was housekeeping."

"And Martin," Mabel said.

"Martin left her alone with the landing," Tessa said. "He did it because he wanted a councillor to like him more than he wanted to stand near Vera while she fussed with ribbon. He will call that public service in his head. It was convenience. It gave her seconds she did not earn."

She wrote one more line in her book, because the day had asked for a clean end.

Window locked: six minutes, blackout. Hale away on call. Vera signed in. Door bolt sings. Receipt clock and phone seconds agree. No more fog.

She shut the book. Outside, the canal took its time the way

it always did. Inside, the kettle clicked. The village held. The seconds sat still on paper. That would have to be enough for tonight.

SIXTEEN

Monday gave the shop a washed light that made edges honest. Ink & Ivy smelled of card stock and the last of Mabel's sponge. Tessa unlocked the small safe, lifted out the hatbox, and set Isla's cup on a square of lintless cloth. Bramble came to rest under the bench with his chin on his paws like a clerk waiting for a line to total.

The handle had cured well under her mix. The seam showed clean, pale along the joint where new met old. No tea in the joint, no stain in the hairline, proof of timing if anyone tried to bluster. She drew the blinds to kill glare and brought the bench lamp down so the light ran across the porcelain like water.

She laid out the little measuring kit she kept for awkward frames and fussy hinges. Calipers. A card protractor cut to mug radius. A thin elastic, the colour of old linen, to mark centre. She looped the elastic around the bowl, lined it with the faint mould seam that ran under glaze from lip through base, and pinned it with two low-tack tabs. The cup knew its midline. She wanted the handle to confess its opinion about it.

Mabel arrived with a mug and an eyebrow that meant she would carry on without being asked. "We are arguing with porcelain," she said.

"We are letting it speak," Tessa said.

She placed the protractor against the elastic at the top of the arc, its zero set to a line she drew down from the cup's centre through the near lip. Then she sighted along the handle's heart line, the small ridge that runs from the heel to the top curl where a finger wants to sit. Handles made for right hands tend to lean a shade clockwise from centre when the maker wants the cup to sit balanced in a right grip, so the wrist need not fight the weight. This handle sat four degrees counterclockwise from the true centre line. Not a huge lean. Enough to tell a hand what to do.

"Left-favouring," Tessa said. "The angle helps a left wrist keep the rim level. A right wrist has to correct."

"Show me with a hand, not numbers," Mabel said.

Tessa did both. She took the cup in her right hand first, keeping the elastic north-south, index at the top curl, thumb over the heel, the way a person lifts for a photograph. The rim wanted to tip. Her wrist had to flex inward to keep the bowl level. Not strain, exactly, but a small fight. She set it down and tried with her left. The rim sat level without argument. Her left thumb found the heel without looking. The curl fitted her index as if the handle had been born there.

She showed Mabel, who felt the same small tug one way and the plain fit the other. Mabel nodded, not delighted, not surprised. "The hand tells the truth when it is not trying to impress anyone," she said.

Tessa took the elastic off and set the cup on a sheet of white card so the rim cast a thin oval. She marked three dots where the lip touched the light and turned the handle five degrees each way, her fingers on the foot for accuracy. The left-lean position kept the rim parallel to the card's baseline without effort when gripped in the left. The right-hand set always wanted a tilt back toward the drinker's chest. She photographed the board, the card, and the protractor, careful with angles and notes on the frame.

"Try the lift test," Mabel said. "One smooth motion to camera height. Right hand first, then left."

Tessa did as asked, both hands steady, both elbows tucked. Her right wrist told the truth in a small way; it tightened across the base of the thumb to pull the rim level in the upward arc. Her left did nothing more than carry weight.

A quick sketch went into her notebook. Cup circle. Centre seam. Handle at minus four degrees. Two little arrows marked R and L with a flat line drawn under the left. No adjectives. No theatre.

"Now the seam," she said, easing closer, eyes on the glue line she had repaired. Whoever had glued on the wrong side for the photographs had done it fast and done it fresh. The old glaze had a soft patina on its edges. The set in the handle heel showed a sharper, newer edge, with micro-scratches from a wipe that had not been there last week. She placed a jeweller's loupe over the heel and breathed slowly. The fresh line ran true for someone who knew clamps and set, but the heel sat a whisper proud on the inside edge, the exact proud you get when a left hand holds the piece while the right dabs and the left sets the angle with the heel of the palm. A right-handed improver would mirror the mistake the other way.

"Pressure comes from the left," she said. "Heel pressed down and inward. You can see the squeeze in the way the adhesive pushes out, thin on the outer arc, a little richer on the inner. The person holding wanted the left to be the boss."

"Your solvent test told you the cap had her bottle," Mabel said. "Now the porcelain tells you the hand had her habit."

Tessa did not answer that at once. She lifted the cup to eye level and watched the handle with the mild ferocity she brought to latches. She pictured a person standing in the hall with Delia flinging list words at them, a table of ribbon near, a camera in the air, a cup in need of speed. A left-dominant set on a family piece because the brain was thinking about the look of a photograph, not about how a bride holds tea.

The bell chimed. Dot from the Barn came in with a reproachful tablet hugged to her front and a plan to be helpful. "Are you allowed to look at the internet," she asked, suspicious of rules. "Because I saw a thing you might want to see."

"We are allowed to look at public boasts," Mabel said. "Sit. Tea."

Dot put the tablet on the counter and opened Vera's warehouse page where the firm posted proof of efficiency to anyone who might book them. Yesterday's post, bragging quietly about a winch that had moved a chandelier without drama, held a carousel of happy images. In the last one, Vera herself stood with a roll of satin held at shoulder height like a banner. Her right hand steadied the roll. Her left made the lift and the pull, which is what mattered. The line at the base of her left thumb shone stark white against the tan, a small pale bar that runs across the thenar when a person has spent years bearing load there. A tendinous crease deepened by pressure, often eased with a strip of tape. In another frame from a week ago, she had indeed worn a thin strip of beige tape in that exact place, the sort sports shops sell to people who refuse to rest.

"Zoom," Tessa said.

Dot pinched the screen. The strain line at the left thumb's base sat clear, the skin around it roughened from solvent. The little flash of adhesive residue on the pad below the line showed as a faint matte patch. In the same frame Vera's right thumb sat smooth, the line shallow, the skin less punished.

"Left hand does the work," Mabel said. "Right hand writes letters. We saw her write with her right. We saw her flip a clipboard with her left. The photos say the same thing louder."

Dot flicked to a short clip where Vera heated a ribbon end with a heat gun for a clean cut. She held the tool in her right hand because the trigger sat right, but she steadied the ribbon with her left and did the pull with the left thumb across the table edge, the exact motion that carves out that pale bar over time.

"Save those," Tessa said. "Print them small and do not get me sued."

Dot printed two stills on the little dye-sub printer she used for donation labels and date tags. She wrote public post on the margin because the Barn liked to point at that word when scolded for curiosity. Then she put the tablet away with the air of someone who had done a kind thing with care.

"Thank you," Tessa said, honest.

Dot beamed and left to meet a woman who had brought in three hats and a reluctant husband.

Tessa took the prints to the bench and placed them beside the card with the elastic and the protractor. She took a clean sheet and drew a hand, quick and neat, left palm up, a bar across the base of the thumb. She wrote strain line here. She wrote left thumb shows chronic loading, solvent dryness. She wrote right thumb smooth. Then she drew the cup again with the handle at minus four degrees and wrote left-dominant set.

Mabel watched, then nudged with a finger. "Write the other line," she said.

"Which one."

"The one about photographs," Mabel said. "She glued for a camera, not a hand."

Tessa wrote it and boxed it because she liked the way a box behaves. Glued for camera, not for use. Left angle sets monogram to face front-left. She had seen it on wedding blogs for years. Left set reads better in shots when the photographer stands left of the aisle. It puts a monogram or a crest toward the lens. Delia would have trained everyone to think like that. Vera already thought like that. Poppy, who lives inside kitchens, would not.

She took one more look at the seam under magnification. There, on the inside elbow of the handle, a tiny smear line followed the curve. Solvent had kissed it before the glue went on. Not enough to bloom the glaze, enough to flash the shine dull for a breath. Jar Four's neat bite. A tidy person wiped the cup before setting the handle. That tidy person made the left angle. The result looked perfect from the left and wrong to any right hand that tried to drink.

Mabel glanced at the clock. "Shaw will like the part where your numbers line up with a photograph," she said. "He will try not to like the part where it smells of psychology."

"He can have it as handwork," Tessa said. "No mind reading. Only thumbs and angles."

She took three photos of the cup with her phone, hands arranged in the same way for both grips, ruler in frame for scale. Then she lifted the elastic off, cleaned the chalk at the pin points, and put the cup back in its nest. The hatbox went to the high shelf with care. Bramble followed the move with holy attention.

They cut through to The Thimble & Fern because tea helps officers make crisp decisions. Shaw had claimed his corner. The pencil still ran his day.

"Your Jar Four page was useful," he said before she opened her mouth. "Cap residue reads alpha terpinene and friends. Our lab likes the way your nose sent them to the correct shelf."

Tessa set down her prints and her card and pushed over the cup photos. "Now for hands," she said. "The handle sits at four degrees left of true. In a left grip the rim stays level. In a right grip the wrist works. The heel shows a tiny proud on the inner, consistent with a left dominant set. There is also a faint solvent scuff under the elbow where a wipe went before the glue. Both speak to a tidy hand that glues for the camera position at the left of the aisle."

Shaw studied the protractor photo with the pedant's satisfaction that had kept him from holes his whole career. "Minus four," he said. "You did not invent a number for effect."

"I do not invent numbers," she said.

He looked at the stills Dot had printed of Vera's hands. He took his time, not for theatre, for care. He traced the pale bar at the base of the left thumb with a fingernail, the skin roughness that years of pulling ribbon and pressing clamps produce. He compared it to the right, smooth and unpunished. He made no noise of triumph.

"Public posts," he said.

"Set yesterday," Tessa said. "And last week. The same line. Left thumb loads, right writes."

He slid the prints under the folder clip, then turned back to the cup photos with the ruler in frame. "You will explain four degrees to a jury with something they can hold," he said.

"I will hold two mugs up and ask them which one fights their wrist," she said. "Then I will set this one where it sat when the camera wanted it and let them see the angle that flatters a lens."

He tapped the solvent scuff on the elbow of the handle in the close shot. "And this," he said.

"A quick wipe before set," she said. "To clean glue residue. The wipe flashes shine off for a second in a thin arc, the same way the cap dulled where a cloth passed. The person holding did it with a habit, not forensics. It is the tidy flourish she does to everything she touches."

Mabel set down tea without being asked. "He will ask where you got the photos," she said. "Say Barn page, public, Dot printed them, and sip like an honest woman."

"Noted," Tessa said.

Shaw wrote four lines on his pad in his careful hand.

Handle left-lean minus 4°. Left wrist natural, right fights. Heel proud inner, left set. Photo evidence, left thumb strain line, solvent dryness.

He underlined left set once and the word photo. "Thank you," he said. "You have a talent for turning a hunch into something that fits on a line."

"It is not a hunch if your thumb feels it," she said.

He stood, pencil behind his ear, a habit that had turned into equipment. "I will speak to Ms Locke," he said. "Not about thumbs. About tools and habits. When she protests, I will show her the cap results and ask her where she stood at nineteen thirty seven and why her name lives in a box she wrote for herself."

When he had gone, the café exhaled. People resumed their concern for scones. Mabel leaned on the counter with both hands flat, content in the way only a clean fact produces.

"You should teach a class," she said. "How to tell a left hand from a right one without being rude."

"I do it with crockery," Tessa said. "It offends fewer people."

Back at the shop, she slid the new prints under the counter glass beside the solvent strip and the blue chalk line. The corner museum now held a tidy run of cause and effect. Citrus peel that dulled a cap. A blue chalk sweep that began on the flat. A saucer's morning starting in a box marked with a warehouse name. A novelty teapot fob and a missing twin. A napkin with minutes. A handle set for a left grip, glued for a lens.

She wrote in her notebook with the ease of a hand that has found its route.

Handle: minus 4° from centre, left-favouring. Right wrist compensates, left carries level. Heel proud inner, squeeze shows left set. Solvent scuff under elbow, quick wipe before glue. Photo:

Vera left thumb strain line and solvent dryness. Writes with right, sets with left.

She added, smaller, glued for camera, not for use. Then she closed the book.

Outside, the canal took its slow silver. Inside, Bramble slept with one paw over his nose, the pose of a dog satisfied with his week's work. The hatbox on the shelf looked calm, as if the cup inside had collected itself for its next appearance. Tessa put the kettle on and thought of a room where a person with neat hands would be asked to tell the truth about them. The truth would not need adjectives. It would have angles, minutes, and the small pale line at the base of a thumb.

SEVENTEEN

By late morning the shop had its steady hum back. The kettle hissed, the bell minded its manners, and the small museum under the counter glass lay in order: brass leaf, ledger stub, Dot's saucer photo, blue chalk line, clock print, solvent strip, napkin times, and the left-lean handle card. Tessa stood at the repair bench and laid out what looked like a small class in adhesives, which in a way it was.

Three brown dropper bottles waited on a tray. Three white tubs sat beside them, each with a flip lid. No labels. A neat row of coffee stirrers. Strips of varnished oak for testing. Two cracked saucers from the odds box that would offend no one if they failed. A stack of lint-free wipes. She had asked Mabel to shuffle everything twice and write the secret key on an index card that now lived under the till.

"Run it past me," Mabel said, setting down two mugs and her most innocent face.

"Three glues," Tessa said. "PVA in Bottle A, cyanoacrylate in Bottle B, epoxy in Bottle C. Three wipes," she added, tapping the tubs. "Plain lemon oil, Jar Two. Catalogue orange remover, Jar Three. CB12 peel, Jar Four. We will not call them that out loud."

"Who are we today," Mabel asked. "Shopkeepers or educators."

"Citizens," Tessa said. "We are choosing a safe wipe for the library tables. We have asked three clever people to advise. One will arrive with a folder."

"Vera loves a folder," Mabel said. "She will smell an unpaid invoice and come running."

Tessa checked the bench one more time, then turned the sign to Open and waited. She did not have to wait long. The bell chimed and Vera Locke appeared with her navy file and a blouse that held its own pleats.

"Ladies," Vera said. "The Inspector raided my week. I thought I would raid yours. I have ten minutes before I make a man cry about bunting."

"You can make him cry here if you prefer," Mabel said. "We are collecting expert opinions for the library. They want a wipe that will lift tape gum and leave old varnish alone. They would also like to know which glue is kind to heirlooms when people insist on playing with handles."

Vera's eyes brightened because a chance to be right in public is a tonic for some people. "Bless your project," she said. "I can spare eight minutes. Then my driver will ring me and tell me he has found a new way to be late."

Tessa gestured to the bench. "We have stripped the labels for fairness," she said. "No brands, only noses and results."

"Fun," Vera said crisply, and set her folder aside without a second thought.

Mabel drifted to the front to soothe a lady with a frame emergency, leaving Tessa and Vera in the good light. Bramble stayed under the bench and pretended he was part of the furniture.

"Glue first," Vera said, already reaching for the droppers with a practised hand. She cracked Bottle B, sniffed once, and smiled. "Thin super," she said. "Good for quick chips, cruel if you flood it." She put a drop on a porcelain shard and pinched it to its partner with the ease of someone who has mended a thousand small tragedies. "You hold this with tape for a minute and a half, then do not breathe near it for ten."

She lifted Bottle C, sniffed, and set it down. "Two-part without the part," she said. "Premixed, slow. I do not like premixes. They lie about shelf life. Fine for a garden pot, not for a cup a grandmother used."

Bottle A she barely sniffed. "PVA," she said. "Polite around paper and frames. Useless on hard glaze unless you are prepared to clamp for a season." She glanced at Tessa's hands. "You know this already. Why am I talking," she said, but she carried on, because talking demonstrated competence and competence is its own coin.

"Now," she said, turning to the tubs. "The room where people ruin furniture. Let me make the mistake for them."

She flipped open the first lid, drew in a small breath, and laughed. "Lemon oil. Smells like a church cupboard. Makes things look honest until a camera sees the streaks. Fine on bare wood that wants comfort. Not for lifting tape."

She opened the second and wrinkled her nose. "Orange solvent. I can smell the propellant even without a spray. It will take sticky off, yes, and then it will sit around bragging about it for an hour. Your library will smell like a fruit market. The tables will resent you."

The third she opened with a small, almost eager move. She bent her head, breathed once, and her mouth tilted. "There you are," she said. "That is the one."

"Which one," Tessa asked, and let her voice sit flat on the counter.

"The peel wipe," Vera said. "The one any sensible person carries in a kit to deal with tape shadow and varnish bloom before a photographer arrives. It flashes and leaves. If you leave it a second too long, it will cut banister varnish and make you swear, but if you are quick it is a dream."

The sentence hung in the air as if it had lines of its own. She had said it lightly, with a small pride in her own skill, as if talking shop. She had said the word banister without being invited to. She had admitted the bite and the fix in one neat claim.

Mabel looked up from the counter as if she had heard a note that did not belong in a tune. She met Tessa's eye and then looked at the far wall with great interest, the way decent people do when facts walk in naked.

Tessa did not blink. "Show me," she said, and placed a varnished strip under the lamp.

Vera dipped a lint wipe into the third tub, tapped once, and drew a clean pass across the strip with the steady wrist of a person who enjoys well-behaved chemicals. The line dulled like a whisper, then was gone. She nodded at her own work.

"Perfect," she said. "You can buff that edge back with a warm cloth if you are fussy, but no one will notice. Use it sparingly. It is dearer than it should be."

"Brand," Tessa said.

Vera tapped the closed lid and smiled without malice. "If I told you I would rob myself of one of the few advantages I have over people who call themselves stylists," she said. "You do not need the brand. You need the habit."

She closed the tub and moved on with the briskness of a woman who keeps time in her head. "Now then, photographs lie. If you do use PVA on a keepsake you want to display, wipe the shine from the squeeze with one of these and let it flash. It saves a glossy bead in the joint. Do not do that on a matte glaze if you like your job."

Tessa watched her hands. Left thumb did the pressure work without thought. Right hand placed and steadied. The small pale bar at the base of the left thumb looked white against the tan from her weekend in a marquee. On the pad below it, a faint matte patch again, a token from solvents that do not care about skin.

"Would you use that wipe on a railing," Tessa asked, setting the question on the table like a sugar bowl. "If you had to lose a smear before a picture."

"On a railing," Vera repeated as if tasting the word. "Only if I had upset the polish with my own cloth and needed to clean my mistake. It bites. It would take the bloom off a banister cap in a heartbeat. Why. Has someone been cleaning the wrong things."

Tessa stirred her tea and wished her heart would learn to ignore days like this. "We are testing theories," she said. "About wipes and the way they behave on old finishes."

"Test your theories on furniture you plan to paint later," Vera advised briskly. "CB peel is for ribbon glue and candle soot. It is not for heirlooms. If you put it on a cap and leave it while you turn to answer a question, you will have a pale ring and a priest."

She laughed to make it a joke. It landed like a stone in a quiet pond.

Mabel set two small saucers on the bench. "One more party trick," she said, breezy. "We have three glues on a line. Pick the one you would use if a bride was breathing down your neck and a photographer wanted to pretend cups never break."

Vera did not even sniff this time. She chose Bottle B, wicked a thread of glue along the fracture, and set the halves with a neat pinch. "That one," she said. "Every time. Clean the squeeze. Tape, then heat if you must. Done."

"Heat," Tessa said mildly.

"Gun on low from a distance," Vera said. "To cure the first minute. Then leave it alone. People want to fuss. Fussing ruins everything."

Tessa sat very still. Heat gun, wipe, quick cure, left thumb pressure. It lined up with Friday's six minutes, Saturday's tidy box, the cap's faint dull, the left-lean handle and the solvent kiss under the elbow. It left room for motive, which would arrive when Martin's messages with trusted partners came home to roost.

Vera snapped the lids closed and checked her watch. "I have to go turn a trestle into a hope," she said. "If the library wants a kit, tell me and I will sell you one at cost because I like books more than chairs."

"We will tell you," Mabel said.

Vera gave Bramble a look a person reserves for a dog who refuses to take sides. He ignored her with grace. She gathered her folder and her certainty and left with the bell singing the note of someone who thinks she has won something.

The shop air changed as soon as she stepped into the lane. Mabel blew out a breath she had been saving.

"She said banister," Mabel said. "Without any help."

"She did," Tessa said.

"And she named the cut," Mabel said. "And the fix. And the heat gun."

"She did," Tessa said again.

"What will we do with our faces when Shaw hears that," Mabel asked.

"Drink tea," Tessa said. "And keep our faces still."

Dot popped her head in as if summoned by fate. "Was that a class," she asked. "It looked useful."

"It was a demonstration," Mabel said. "We learned that some people cannot resist showing off when a bench is tidy."

Dot nodded, wise. "I will write that down," she said, and

vanished.

Tessa tidied the bench with care. She put lids back on. She set the test strip aside, labelled, and noted the pass Vera had drawn so cleanly. She wrote the sentence as it had fallen from Vera's mouth, exactly, without embroidery. That one cuts banister varnish. She added, said lightly, no prompt. She added, identified CB by scent and effect with labels hidden.

Then she rang Shaw.

He came within twenty minutes, which counted as haste for a man who likes to arrive after the adjectives have left. He listened to the set-up without interruption, read the notes, and stood at the bench as if it were a witness.

"You stripped the labels," he said.

"We did," Tessa said.

"She still found the peel," he said.

"She did," Tessa said.

"And she said what," he asked.

"That one cuts banister varnish," Tessa said. "And told us how not to get caught by our own wipe."

He rubbed the side of his jaw with the end of his pencil, a habit he might break one day if the pencil broke first. "You did not mention rails," he said.

"I asked about a railing after," Tessa said. "She called it a banister. She volunteered the bite. She set a line about priests."

"Priests," he repeated, amused despite himself. "Good. She is tidy even in jokes."

Mabel put the test strip under the lamp and showed him the dull bar left by Jar Four's pass. She did it with the pride of a woman who keeps evidence neat for supper.

"She drew that line," Mabel said. "Eyes shut, practically."

Shaw watched the light catch the dulled grain and nodded once. "The lab liked your terpinene," he said. "Now I have a sentence I can say in a room. Ms Locke identifies a brand by scent with labels covered and then admits its effect on varnish. I do enjoy a room that goes quiet."

He took the tubs, numbered and taped, into his bag with a label and a date. He took the test strip in a sleeve. He took Tessa's note with the quoted line and her neat annotation. He did not take the cracked saucer, which pleased Tessa; she wanted one thing in the room she could mend that did not speak.

"Thank you," he said. "Tomorrow we will convene. Today I will let her write her own ending on a form."

He left to do that particular work. The bell made its polite sound. The lane went back to small business and bikes. The canal offered a glint that meant little and improved the window anyway.

Mabel poured tea because the body needs a ritual after truth. "You feel satisfied," she said.

"I feel tidy," Tessa said. "Which is a trap. We are not done."

"No," Mabel said. "But we are holding the right thread and the end feels close enough to see."

Tessa wrote three spare lines in her book.

Decoy at bench. Three glues, three wipes, labels hidden. Vera picked CB by scent, said lightly it cuts banister varnish if left a beat. Demonstrated quick pass, dull flash. Named heat gun for first minute cure.

She added, smaller, left thumb did pressure work, solvent dryness on pad. Then she slid the page under the counter glass.

Bramble sighed and rolled to show his ribs as if he had carried the morning on his back. Tessa obliged with a scratch. The hatbox on the high shelf looked untroubled at last. The seam held. The handle sat true. Some things accept repair and behave. Others need a room, a sentence, and the right silence after it lands.

EIGHTEEN

Fernvale Hall wore its Sunday best as if manners could cancel gravity. The chairs made neat rows. The urns at the doors stood at attention. Len had set a long trestle along the side wall and covered it with brown paper like a school experiment. On it sat the small choir of objects Tessa had gathered all week. Chalked parchment in a sleeve. A varnished test strip. A print of Dot's photograph. A copy of the outage sheet. A photo of a novelty teapot fob with the nick. The protractor card with the handle angle. Two small stills from Vera's public posts showing a left thumb with a pale bar. Nothing flashy. Everything exact.

Detective Inspector Shaw stood near the trestle with his pencil and his stillness. Constable Hargreaves had planted himself by the side doors with the look of a man who knew how to remove a person without turning it into theatre. Mabel had a clipboard she did not need and the kind of cardigan that calmed rooms.

Vera Locke came with a navy folder that held its corners like a standard. Martin Hale arrived with his jacket off and the confidence of a man who knew where the good light fell. Poppy Hartley sat with her mother, hands locked under one thigh so they would not leap up and try to fix the day. Len stayed on his feet by the corridor door as if he owed the hinges an apology. Sian had been given a chair near the back and used it to write neat notes she would not be asked for. One Laurel Trust trustee turned up, Mr Fairchild, with a face that said he preferred committee rooms to halls with history in the air.

Shaw did not bang a table. He looked at the room until it went quiet on its own. "Thank you for coming," he said. "We will stay civil. Ms Harper will lay out the facts and the order in which they speak. Keep your comments to when I ask for them. If you talk over her, I will talk over you."

He turned to Tessa and nodded once. The trestle waited. The room breathed.

Tessa set her hand on the first sleeve, the chalked parchment. "We start at the landing," she said. "This is a print from a controlled test on the flat section before the stair. The smears you see are signatures from three soles. A natural stride leaves a clean transfer that stops before the nosing. A poor step at the lip makes a drag that begins at the edge. The dark sweep that shows here begins forty centimetres back from the lip. That is where our slide began. Not on the top stair. On the flat. A push or a sharp unbalance sends a body into that run. A stumble at the lip does not."

She did not look at anyone yet. She let the sheet do the speaking it had done for her. "The lab has the original," she said. "Constable Hargreaves witnessed the collection. The start on the flat is the fact that removes accident from the front line."

She lifted the second piece. A small varnished strip with a single dull bar across it. "This is a pass from a citrus wipe on old varnish," she said. "It flashes, dulls cleanly, then leaves little scent. The lab reads alpha terpinene and friends, which is what a certain brand of peel wipe leaves when it behaves. On the banister cap at the landing, the lab found the same signature. There is no lemon oil on that cap. There is no kitchen. There is this."

Shaw did not move, but the fine muscles in his face agreed with the sentence. Vera kept her chin level. Martin watched the strip as if numbers might appear on it and rescue him.

"On Friday night," Tessa went on, "the hall ran a blackout rehearsal for ambience. Skylight dimmers lowered the light between nineteen thirty two and thirty nine. The mains cut for a minute at nineteen forty one. The back corridor door bolt sensor logged two movements during the dim: nineteen thirty two and eleven seconds, and nineteen thirty five and fifty four. Len opened at nineteen thirty two. The second belongs to a different ring."

She set the outage sheet beside a print of the sensor log, the numbers underlined once in black. "Mr Hale took a call at nineteen thirty five," she said. "His call log shows it. It ended at nineteen forty one and three seconds. He walked with Inspector Shaw from his office door to the landing yesterday. It took thirty two seconds. That gives a window of six minutes in which the landing lived in grey without Mr Hale beside it."

She did not need to say a name for the next step. She placed the blue folder open to Friday's sign-in page under the lamp. Vera's neat capitals were a picture. 19:34, anteroom. Time out blank. "Ms Locke wrote herself into the corridor at nineteen thirty four," Tessa said. "She wrote a box for Saturday morning as well. Nine fifty eight to ten oh six. Same hand. The Saturday box was added late. Ruler dent here. Len's pen. These are not guesses. They live on paper."

She turned Dot's small glossy print so the room could see it. The Locke & Linen box sat on the Barn trolley at nine twelve with a white saucer on top. The hairline in the glaze showed, clean and familiar. Gareth Pike's sleeve read LOCKE in block letters. "This is the saucer Isla thought lost," Tessa said. "It sat on top of a box from Ms Locke's warehouse at nine twelve. The hall crate arrived at the Barn at nine twenty eight, which the bell remembers. By noon, the saucer sat on that crate, which our photograph shows. We are not accusing the Barn. Gwen moved like to like later because she is tidy and it looked right. The chain begins with Locke. Not with the hall."

Vera's folder shifted a fraction under her hand. She did not reach for it. She looked at Dot's print as if it might try to prove it had been somewhere else and needed to be told not to.

Tessa set the protractor card down. The elastic loop marked the cup's centre line. The handle line sat four degrees left of true. She put the two stills from Vera's public posts beside it. The pale bar at the base of the left thumb sat starker under the hall light.

"The handle on Isla's family cup was glued for a left grip," she said. "Minus four degrees from centre. A left wrist lifts level without effort. A right wrist must correct. The heel sits a shade proud on the inner, which is what you see when a left hand sets the angle and presses. Under the elbow you can see a faint solvent scuff where a wipe had kissed the glaze before the glue. Ms Locke's left thumb shows chronic load and solvent dryness. She writes with her right, she sets with her left. On Saturday, she chose the peel wipe by scent in my shop without a label on the jar and joked that it cuts banister varnish if you let it sit. We recorded the sentence. She said it lightly. She did not know where we were going."

Silence held. It felt earned, not forced. Poppy's mother took her daughter's hand again, not to steady her, to stop herself rising.

Tessa returned each item to its place in the neat line. Then she looked up and let her eyes take the room in order. "Friday," she said, "was the rehearsal. The dimmer run and Mr Hale's phone call gave Ms Locke six minutes on the landing in low light, signed in by her own hand at nineteen thirty four. You test a bite like that in grey. You feel how a cap behaves when it is clean and a peel has flashed across it. You tell yourself you are tidying. You teach your palm what a slide feels like."

She did not soften the next bit. "Saturday morning was the performance. Ms Locke added a vendor box to the outage sheet in tidy print that put her in the anteroom from nine fifty eight to ten oh six. That window lives on the board now. During that time she could wipe the cap with the same peel. It dulls, it leaves. It makes a hand miss for a moment before it grips. At eleven oh nine, when Delia took the turn, the landing was slick from Len's pride and the cap did not help. The skid begins on the flat. The push starts there."

Len swallowed. He did not try to defend his pride. He looked at the varnished strip and nodded once to it as if accepting a lesson from a piece of wood.

Shaw let the pause sit long enough for the fact to find a chair in every head. Then he said, "Speak to motive."

Tessa kept her voice level. "Ms Locke lost the Fernvale wedding account to Delia this season. That cost hurt her in profit and in pride. Mr Hale had been pressing the Laurel Trust to keep events at the hall and to package contracts under one vendor to please sponsors. His emails use the phrase single source. Ms Locke's brochures use trusted partners in the same place. The two of you spent Friday morning tuning a sponsorship pack, and Friday night on a dimmer run. Saturday morning Ms Locke wrote her own slot onto an official sheet and signed herself into the corridor. Delia Hartley stood in her way in the most public sense Remove the planner, and Locke & Linen stands ready to fill the gap on paper as a partner the Trust can present as efficient."

Martin cleared his throat with care. "That is a dramatic set," he said, which was his way of saying it sounded plausible and he disliked it. "You have not shown me a line from my office that says hire Ms Locke for the next decade."

"You wrote enough for a reader to see where you wanted to go," Shaw said, dry and courteous. "We will read the rest of your messages with pleasure. We will also enjoy the locksmith's notes about the duplicate you had on your desk. You do not have to push a person to be inside this story. You only have to steer rooms so a person like Ms Locke can arrive first and leave last."

Vera raised her chin. "You cannot put me on a landing at eleven oh nine," she said. "Your own fuel slip and your dash camera flirt with a station. Your own timeline puts me at Mr Hale's office at eleven thirty. Your own café tape shows his water at ten twenty eight. I am not your push."

Shaw did not bristle. "We have not said you stood on the stair at eleven oh nine," he said. "We have said you prepared the cap so a hand seeking safety would not find it. We have said you were alone on that landing during the dimmer rehearsal and alone in that corridor during the vendor box you wrote. We have said your wipe speaks on the cap. We have said you identify it by scent without a label. We have said the handle was set left by a left hand in love with speed and photos. Push and polish can be separate acts that agree with one another."

Vera let out a small breath. "You will have your lab tricks. You will have your pretty speech. You will not have a motive that survives daylight. I do not murder for contracts. I win them."

"You do both," Tessa said, still calm. "You win and you punish. Delia refused Poppy a letter for a loan. You felt it as a similar snub. You told Len to move a sign. You tidy people when they get in your way. This time you tidied a handhold."

Poppy stood before anyone could stop her. "She told me to get a hobby," she said. "My sister's planner. To my face. I did not push her down a stair for it. I am right handed and I can live with humiliation. She did not like being told no. She never learned how."

Vera turned toward her, ready with a sentence that would

rearrange the air. Shaw lifted a hand a fraction and she thought better of testing it.

Mr Fairchild coughed in the manner of trustees who like minutes. "Inspector," he said. "Do you have this solvent of theirs in a bag."

"I do," Shaw said. "Numbered, sealed, and already kissed by a lab. We will not pass it round like chutney."

"Good," Mr Fairchild said, brisk. "I have heard the argument and do not require the smell to take a view."

Len found his voice again. "I know what I did," he said to Shaw. "I want it recorded. I ran my own polish for cash. I moved the sign. I put shine where a shoe has no business skating. I let a neat person write into my book. I did not push a soul. I will eat this in public if it helps the rest of you eat the truth."

"It helps," Shaw said. "You will still pay a small fine to a small court for the mop. You will survive it with your pride still tiresome."

"Fair," Len said.

Sian lifted one hand without standing. "If you need Mr Hale's call log on paper," she said, "I have already printed the page. If you need the trust's procurement memo with the words single source struck out and trusted partners written in the margin, I have that too. I am tired of watching a phrase change clothes on the way to a brochure."

Martin looked at her, not angry, tired. "Thank you, Sian," he said. "Bring the file. It is time the board read the minutes they thought they wrote."

The air in the room shifted. You could feel when paper decided to side with light. Shaw nodded to Hargreaves. "Collect Ms Hughes's bundle," he said. "Sign for it."

He turned back to the trestle. "Ms Harper," he said. "Anything else."

"One small thing," Tessa said. She picked up the cracked saucer she had mended as a demonstration and laid it beside the protractor card. "When I invited Ms Locke to advise the library on wipes, she chose the peel by scent with the labels covered and said the line about banisters. She reached for cyanoacrylate without looking and said heat gun for the first minute. Her left thumb did the pressure job while the right played foreman. That small scene was not a trap. It was a mirror. She behaved here the way she behaves everywhere."

Vera smiled with scant warmth. "And you behaved with the smugness of a woman who thinks hobby shops are courtrooms," she said. "Congratulations. You fixed a saucer. Do you plan to fix the world."

"I plan to write minutes," Tessa said. "The world will do as it likes."

Shaw closed his folder. "That is enough for today," he said. "The physicals will do their bit in the morning. We will ask for your devices and your clothes from Friday night and Saturday morning, Ms Locke. Mr Hale, we will ask for your messages with the words partner, package, single, source, and canal. Bring patience. Do not leave the county."

Martin's jaw set at the last word. Vera's fingers tightened on her folder, then relaxed as if she had told them to.

Poppy's mother rose and thanked nobody and everybody for sitting without shouting. Len took the bucket handle and left it where it belonged, empty. Mr Fairchild wrote something concise that he would later call a note. Sian handed Hargreaves a sealed envelope and looked as if a width had come off her shoulders. Mabel collected the trestle kit with the efficiency of a woman who has wrapped up fetes before anyone noticed the bunting had started to sag.

When the room thinned, Shaw stood with Tessa at the landing and looked at the cap without touching it. The dull had faded to a whisper. The handprints left by visitors today sat further along the rail where good manners lead them. Gravity had done nothing new in the last hour.

"Thank you," he said. "You kept adjectives out of a tricky room."

"I am saving them for tea," she said.

"Do not drink tea with Ms Locke," he said. "She will pour it over your notes and call it an accident."

He went to his car with the folder under his arm and the pencil behind his ear. Tessa packed the sleeves and the prints, the protractor and the strip, into the box that had carried them in. Bramble waited at the door with his harness on his nose and an air of service.

On Ivy Lane, the day had the colour of clean porcelain. Ink & Ivy smelled of paper and good glue. The small museum under the counter glass gained one more line written in neat hand on a card no bigger than a biscuit.

Room laid out: slide starts on flat, cap wears peel, saucer starts in Locke box, vendor window, six minutes in dim, duplicate key, handle set left. Motive: contracts steered, revenge for the lost account.

She slid the card into place and put the kettle on. Mabel counted out two cups, one for truth and one for patience. Outside, the canal said nothing helpful and kept its word.

NINETEEN

Morning brought a clean, workmanlike light to Fernvale. Ink & Ivy breathed paper and calm. Tessa set the Open sign at a practical angle and checked the small museum under the counter glass. The blue chalk strip. Dot's saucer photo with the 9:12 stamp. The solvent test. The napkin times copied onto a straight card. The teapot fob with the nick. The handle angle at minus four degrees. Everything sat where it could speak without being asked.

Mabel topped up the biscuit tin and called it a hedge against trouble. Bramble took up his post beside the till with noble economy of movement. At ten the bell sounded and Constable Hargreaves came in with his neatness and a message.

"Inspector asks if you will step to the hall," he said. "He will show his homework. If you do not mind being an audience."

"We never mind that," Mabel said.

They crossed Ivy Lane with Bramble carrying himself as if on parade. Fernvale Hall looked scrubbed by purpose. Chairs set straight for no one, doors propped, a notice on the foyer table that read Room in use. Len hovered by the office as if doors needed chaperoning. He nodded to them, grateful and wearing penance like a waistcoat.

Shaw had taken the long trestle again. He had added a few things. Clear wallets with labels. A small black case from the lab. A folded printout that had Sian's neat hand on the cover. He looked as he always did when a line had stopped being an idea and become a plank under his feet.

"Thank you for coming," he said. "We will keep this short."

Vera arrived with her folder and her fixed calm. Martin came a minute later with his jacket over his arm like a man who had changed his shirt for a meeting. Sian slipped in behind him, chin set. Mr Fairchild of the trustees stood with a notebook at a distance that suggested he would like to be anywhere else. Poppy's mother stayed by the back row in case the day tried to run away from itself.

Hargreaves took up position by the side door and gave the room the look that warns people not to turn a page too fast. Shaw did not raise his voice. He placed a single sheet in the centre of the trestle and began.

"First," he said, "the cap."

He lifted the lab report from its wallet and did not let it flap. "The banister cap at the landing carried a faint residue. Gas chromatography shows alpha terpinene, gamma terpinene, limonene, and small friends in the same ratios as a commercial citrus peel wipe. No lemon oil, no beeswax, no household polish. The same profile appears on the wipe pack seized from Ms Locke's kit. There is also micro-varnish on the pack's underside, flakes under fifty microns, with a resin signature consistent with the French polish used on Fernvale's rail. We took a control shaving from the rail underside with Mr Porter's consent. Spectra match. That pack sat on this cap or on a surface that wore the same varnish within the last forty-eight hours."

Vera kept her face still. It had taken practice to make it do that. She looked at Shaw and made no bid for the floor.

"Second," Shaw said, "the heat gun."

He opened the black case and set a clear bag down. Inside sat a nozzle guard from a compact gun and three swabs in tubes. "Your warehouse gun, Ms Locke," he said. "The nozzle guard shows a faint film that carries the same terpenes as the wipe, likely from your habit of cleaning tools with your own cloths. There is also cyanoacrylate deposition on the guard, which we would expect given your method of pushing a first cure. None of that would interest me much on its own. What interests me is that the film on the guard carried a trace of the same shellac-based varnish as the cap flakes. Not enough for a man to make poetry about. Enough for me to say this tool went near a banister or a similar finish after a peel. You were very tidy on Saturday. Your tools kept a memory you did not mean them to keep."

Vera's folder edge made a small shave in the air as she tightened her hand. She did not speak.

"Third," he said, "the handle."

He tapped the protractor card and the close shot of the solvent kiss under the elbow. "Minus four degrees from centre. Left set, heel proud on the inner. Solvent scuff on the elbow consistent with a quick wipe before glue. Not a kitchen smell. The same peel. Your public post shows your left thumb loaded, your right smooth. You picked the peel by scent without a label yesterday. You told us it cuts banister varnish if you leave it a beat. We will play that part of Ms Harper's note if you contradict me."

He did not wait for contradiction. He moved to the next wallet.

"Fourth," he said, "the saucer chain of custody."

He held up Dot's photograph and read the time. "Nine twelve," he said. "Locke box on the Barn trolley. Saucer on top. Gareth Pike's sleeve in frame. Hall crate bell at nine twenty eight. Saucer photographed on Hall crate by eleven forty eight. Ms Locke, your driver brought a box with that saucer on top before Ms Hartley fell. You can tell me why a matching saucer walked into your lorry if you like. You can also tell me why you added a vendor window to the outage sheet at nine fifty eight with a ruler and your neat capitals."

He set the outage sheet beside the sign-in page. The tidy print glared under the hall lights. Friday's 19:34 anteroom line with the blank out box. Saturday's 09:58 to 10:06 in the same hand.

"Fifth," he said, "the window."

He read the indecently exact time stamps from the back corridor bolt sensor. "Nineteen thirty two and eleven. Nineteen thirty five and fifty four," he said. "Mr Hale answered a call at nineteen thirty five and walked back at nineteen forty one and thirty five when I made him do it yesterday. During that six-minute dim, you were signed into the corridor, Ms Locke. You had the landing. Mr Hale had a call. Ms Hartley had a habit of patting the cap. Mr Porter had put too much pride on the floor."

He let the sheet sit and then turned to Martin with the same quiet care.

"Now the messages," he said.

Sian's packet lay ready. Shaw lifted the cover and took out two printed chains and a memo. He placed them in order like a person setting the pieces for a hand of cards.

"To the trustees' WhatsApp group," he said, tapping the first. "From you, Mr Hale, on Wednesday last. 'If we package events through one trusted partner we look more credible to Laurel. Single source looks cleaner on paper.' Reply from Mr Fairchild: 'Single source sounds like risk in procurement. Rephrase.' Your reply: 'Call it trusted partners. Same idea.' And here," he said, tapping the second chain, "to Ms Locke at ten oh nine on

Friday morning. 'Let us tune the sponsorship copy to highlight continuity suppliers. Trustees will back us if we can show a joined-up approach. I can steer this if you carry the setup.' Her reply: 'Always happy to carry what someone else drops.'"

Martin's temper held, then faltered, then remembered itself. He took a breath that sounded like patience rubbing its hands.

"That is not a crime," he said. "That is stewarding. We push for a partner framework all the time. We make papers consistent. We chase language. It is how halls survive."

"It is also how a planner finds herself edged out of a season if she refuses to play," Shaw said. "And when the planner falls, the framework is ready. We will let the court draw a line between your helpful language and the irregular steps that make it corruption. You used your role to steer work. You forgot to write it down in the right places."

Mr Fairchild looked older by a year. "We will convene," he said to no one in particular. "And not in a fortnight. Today."

Shaw put his pencil down as if that small act had weight. "Ms Locke," he said, turning back, "you are under arrest on suspicion of murder. We will caution you now. You do not have to say anything. If you do not say something you later rely on in court, it may go against you. Anything you do say will be used in evidence."

Vera's stillness did not crack so much as shift its footing. Her left thumb moved over the pad of her finger and left a faint pale mark when she pressed. She looked at Tessa as if the world had been badly arranged and the wrong person had been put in charge of glue.

"I did not push her," she said, voice clean. "I cleaned a smear. That is all. People are clumsy."

"You cleaned the cap so a hand would miss," Tessa said, quiet. "And you did it knowing the landing sat like glass."

Vera's jaw lifted. "Everyone in this room cleans for photographs," she said. "You are not better than me because you like books."

Shaw did not trade opinions. He nodded to Hargreaves. Hargreaves stepped forward with cuffs that had nothing theatrical about them. Vera put her wrists out without making it a scene. She looked at Martin once as if to see whether the wind could be persuaded to blow the other way. It could not. She looked back at Shaw.

"You will not hold a contract if you make villains out of suppliers," she said to Martin, and then to Shaw, "I will beat this on paper."

Shaw met her eye. "Paper is not your friend today," he said.

Hargreaves led her out without hurry. The hall did that strange thing where sound drops and then comes back in a different shape. Poppy's mother gripped the back of a chair and let her shoulders ease by small degrees. Len put his pen down and looked at his hands as if they had surprised him by being honest at last.

Shaw turned to Martin. He did not alter his tone.

"Mr Hale," he said, "you are under arrest on suspicion of misconduct in public office and corruption. You used your position to steer Laurel Trust work toward a favoured supplier. We will caution you as well."

Martin did not put his hands out at once. He had not expected cuffs. He had expected a note on letterhead and a lecture. Then he remembered who he was standing in front of and who had kept the notes this week. He set his jaw, lifted his wrists, and accepted the metal like an unpleasant fact.

"You can save yourself and this hall some trouble if you come clean on the duplicate key," Shaw said. "We have it back. I still require your own words for when you took it and why you thought you could put it on your desk and call it a system."

"That is petty," Martin said, weary.

"That is how we get through doors," Shaw said.

Sian stood very straight. She did not cry. She stepped forward with a folder that held every unflattering thing Martin had asked her to type in the last month and handed it to Hargreaves. Mr Fairchild put his hand on her shoulder with a care that looked real.

"Thank you," he said to her, simply.

Martin looked at his secretary, then at the floor, then at the cap as if it might speak for him. It did not. He let Hargreaves take his arm and did not argue when asked to leave his phone and his watch on the trestle. He left as Vera had, without fuss. The door shut with more courtesy than either of them had shown the week.

Shaw exhaled. It was not dramatic. It was only human.

"That is the ugly work," he said to the room. "We will do the tidy work now. Statements. Locks. Minutes."

He turned to Len. "Mr Porter, we will take your confession about cash and polishing to the local bench. They will fine you enough to sting and leave you free enough to keep your job if the trustees have sense. They will also ask you to learn to love a label maker."

"I am already in love," Len said, throat rough.

Shaw looked at Poppy and her mother. "I am sorry for your week," he said. "I am sorrier for your loss. Everything else is noise."

Poppy nodded once, steady. "Thank you," she said. "I did not push her. I did throw a fork in the sink and scare the cat. I am not proud of that."

"No one is proud this week," Mabel said, and took her hand for a second. "Have tea with us later. We will not ask you any clever questions."

Mr Fairchild removed his spectacles, cleaned them with a handkerchief, and put them back on as if that simple act could restore sense. "This hall owes people apologies," he said. "We will write them and read them properly. We will also call a locksmith this afternoon."

"You will also write your procurement framework like grown-ups," Shaw said. "And you will stop writing lovely words to hide ugly habits."

Mr Fairchild did not argue. "Yes," he said.

The hall released them slowly, as if it wanted to keep them until everyone had filled a form. Outside, Ivy Lane looked smaller in the honest light. Mabel took Tessa's arm like a friend and not a co-worker and they walked back to the shop with Bramble in a mood to heel for a living.

Inside Ink & Ivy, Tessa put the kettle on with hands that kept steady and clear. She took a clean card and wrote the day's last proofs in straight lines.

Lab: terpinene profile on cap. Same profile on Vera's wipe pack. Micro-varnish on pack underside matches Fernvale rail. Heat gun nozzle guard carries peel residue and shellac trace, plus CA deposition. Handle left-set, solvent scuff under elbow. Saucer at 09:12 on Locke box, bell 09:28 hall crate. Friday sign-in 19:34 V. Locke, anteroom. Back corridor bolts at 19:32:11 and 19:35:54. Hale call 19:35–19:41:03. Six-minute window. Messages: Hale steering, single source to trusted partners. Arrests made.

She slid the card under the counter glass with the others and stood looking at the small museum until her eyes settled.

Mabel leaned on the counter. "You look as if you have been running," she said.

"I have been counting," Tessa said. "It uses the same muscles."

Bramble flopped on his side and presented his ribs for light duty. Tessa obliged with absent-minded kindness. The bell chimed and Sian came in with an unbrave laugh and a request.

"May I sit for five minutes and not be anyone's sensible person," she asked.

"You may sit for fifteen," Mabel said, ushering her to a chair as if it were a ferry.

Sian took the tea Mabel put in her hand and stared at the sugar bowl as if it told fortunes. "He asked me to change single source to trusted partners," she said. "As if a coat matters when your shirt is dirty. I typed it. I am not proud of that."

"You printed it," Tessa said. "That is the difference. You chose paper over pride."

Sian breathed out, then in, then out again, as if changing air. "Thank you," she said, and drank with both hands.

A boy came in for a pack of blue card and left with the feeling he had been part of something important by accident. The canal outside did its slow silver business. The day made reasonable progress.

At noon, Shaw came to the door without ceremony. He looked as if he had put his pencil down for a minute and missed it. Mabel gave him a sandwich from a tin without asking what he wanted. He accepted it as if it had always been coming.

"Physicals will please the Crown," he said, almost cheerful. "The varnish on the pack makes my week. I could have done without the heat gun, but I am not ungrateful. We also have the garment bag from Ms Locke's van. The cuff carries a speck of the same shellac and a ghost of peel. I will not make a fuss about the cuff. I will keep it for dessert."

"Martin," Tessa asked.

"On his way to interview," he said. "He may claim zeal. He may say he wrote vigorous emails in the name of a hall he loves. He will sit in a room and hear the number of times he wrote steer and package. The key nonsense will not help him. His board will be short one chair for a bit."

He ate half the sandwich and put the other half in his pocket like a responsible person. He looked at the counter museum and tapped the corner of the solvent photo with a knuckle.

"You kept me honest," he said. "I like being right. I prefer to be right for the right reasons."

"You keep me legal," she said. "I like puzzles. I prefer not to play at court."

He nodded, took his pencil back out of wherever he had tucked it, and left again to spend the afternoon with statements and rooms without windows.

After he had gone, Tessa wrote one more neat line under the glass.

Shaw presented the physicals. Varnish on her pack. Peel on the cap. Peel on her tool. Messages about steering. Vera arrested for murder. Martin arrested for corruption.

She put the pen down and stood still with the comfortable heaviness that arrives when a set of facts stops fighting. The hatbox on the high shelf looked content, the seam holding, the handle set true. Bramble snored the way dogs do when the world has returned to boring, which is their preferred state.

"Tea," Mabel said.

"Tea," Tessa agreed.

They drank it hot, properly, in a room that smelled of paper and clean glue. Outside, the canal carried on. Inside, the week turned a page without creasing it. Tomorrow would be for the quiet end and the whisper of something else behind it. Today had done the close.

Got it. Here's the final chapter with a warm close at Ink & Ivy, tea with Mabel and Lin, Bramble asleep, and the arc seed paid off: the brass tab and ledger stub read Canal Gate, phase one. Tessa keeps them tucked away. Shaw clocks it, says nothing, and leaves a quiet promise to look into the Trust.

TWENTY

Evening took the edge off Fernvale. Ink & Ivy held the kind of calm a shop earns by keeping its counters clean and its kettle honest. The hatbox sat high, the family cup settled, its handle true. Paper smelled of paper. Glue minded its manners. Bramble slept with his muzzle on his paws, tail ticking now and then as if contentment needed marking.

Mabel brought a plate of shortbread from the tin that keeps morale steady. Lin arrived with a bundle of rosemary and the last of his pears, trousers marked with the day's soil, smile clean. He set the herbs by the window and the pears in the blue bowl, then took a chair that had a fine view of the kettle.

"To endings," he said. "And to the sort of beginning we only admit out loud after cake."

"Tea first," Mabel said, pouring. "People say fate, but it is tea."

They ate in the sifting quiet that comes when a village decides it has talked enough for one day. Sian passed the window on her way home and lifted a hand, a small salute that said the heavy part had been carried to the right room. Len's cap bobbed past after that, set at a better angle, a label maker box under his arm like penance that might be fun if he let it.

"Trust will be in a meeting for weeks," Lin said, stirring. "Mr Fairchild walked across the green with a notebook and the look of a man who has found his grown-up voice. That normally takes a funding crisis or an aunt."

"Or a landing," Mabel said.

Tessa let herself be still. The rush had gone. The thinking had not. She wiped her hands on the linen towel that always lived by the kettle, then crossed to the back room and unlocked the small safe.

The glassine envelopes sat where she had left them. The brass tab waited, no bigger than a postage stamp, laurel leaf pressed clean, a pinhole punched for a ring. The ledger stub lay beside it, torn from a book that would have been proud of its columns. She eased the stub into the light, set a ruler along the edge, and read what had bothered her since Saturday.

CANAL GATE, PHASE ONE, written on the top line in a hand that liked neatness for public documents. Below it, numbers in two columns and the sort of abbreviations committees use when they feel brisk. Hire, lighting, stewarding, plaque run, with a total that sat higher than it had any right to. In the corner, a small lemon smear that would have gone unnoticed if not for the week. She tucked that thought away for later. The words were enough for tonight.

Mabel stood beside her, eyes level with the paper. "Phase one," she said. "There is always a phase two in that tone."

"And a phase three if nobody stops them," Lin added, not unkind, only practical. "The Gate pays for anything if you say heritage twice and add a leaflet."

"Tab," Tessa said, and showed him the small brass leaf. He nodded at once.

"Plaque set," he said. "They hang these from hooks when the order goes out. I have seen the crates in the Trust office. Leaves to screw on boards, one for each donor who wants proof they exist."

Tessa slid the tab back into its sleeve, then the stub, then the two together into a heavier envelope. She closed the safe, then paused with her hand on the lid. In the shop's front room, Fernvale's small noises went on, old wood ticking, kettle settling, Bramble's breath even.

The bell chimed once. Shaw stepped in with his pencil behind his ear and a face that belonged to a man who had spoken to solicitors all afternoon without letting it spoil him. He removed his hat, because he was that sort, and offered Mabel a quiet thank you when she poured for him without asking.

"Housekeeping," he said, taking a seat. "Ms Locke is in a place with walls that do not flatter. Mr Hale has remembered he is a citizen. The trustees are busy being worthy. Your community will recover faster than its inbox."

"Good," Mabel said. "We prefer ordinary."

Shaw's gaze drifted to the back room door for a second, the way it always did when paper lived there. Tessa did not move to block his view. She is not the blocking kind. She only lifted the envelope from the safe and set it on the counter in plain sight.

"Found on the repair bench," she said. "Saturday. Brought in a spool of old ribbon. Brass laurel tab. Ledger stub with Canal Gate, phase one. Numbers too fat for comfort. I have not paraded it through the square."

Shaw looked at the envelope and then at her, taking the measure of what she was offering and what she meant to hold back for now. He did not reach. He did not lecture. He had spent the day telling people precisely what to do. He was content to leave one thing where it was.

"Keep it," he said. "Keep it dry and dull. I will come for it when the trustees finish arguing with their mirrors."

Lin smiled into his cup. "That is a gardener's promise," he said. "Water later, not now."

Shaw took that with a nod. "If any of you hear the words Phase Two spoken in a bright voice, tell me before anyone prints a brochure," he added. "I would like to get ahead of the next problem without a stair in it."

"We will tell you if anyone starts measuring a plaque board," Mabel said. "Or if Martin writes cohesion with his left hand."

Shaw almost smiled. He finished his tea and, because politeness had not left him yet, set the cup edge straight on the saucer before he stood.

"Tessa," he said at the door, low enough that it belonged to the three of them. "You were right about the cap, the window, the handle, and the habit. If you decide to be wrong next week, do it about cake. It costs less sleep."

"I will be wrong about icing," she said.

He gave Bramble a dignified nod, which the dog ignored with grace, then left without fuss. The bell found its polite note and let the lane back in.

Lin put the rosemary on the sill and the shop filled with the clean edge that herb always brings. Mabel cut a slice of something plain and good, set plates out, and stopped the day before it drifted toward worry.

"Tell us what we are looking at tomorrow," she said.

"Glass and quiet," Tessa said. "I have three frames who think they are eccentrics. I will make them behave. After that, I might teach the village how to label hooks without losing its soul."

Lin leaned back until his chair found the sweet spot. "I will mend the post by the Gate," he said. "With screws that do not rust. The trustees can call it Phase Zero and bill no one."

They ate. They talked about rosemary and bees and a robin with thoughts above its station. The shop took on the soft tiredness of a place that has earned it. People went by the window and did not peer in for once, respecting an evening they could not name but understood.

When the light had thinned to the colour of good paper, Tessa washed the cups, dried them, and set them in their stack the way she always did, handle right, rim unchipped. She checked the bolt, clicked the sign to Closed, and stood a moment with her hand on the door as the canal took its slow silver.

In the back room she opened the safe again and looked at the envelope once more, not because she doubted it, because looking fixes things. Brass leaf. Ledger line. Canal Gate, phase one. She added a card on top, her neat print holding its place.

Hold for Shaw. Trust thread. Do not let it wander.

She closed the safe and turned the key. Bramble rolled onto his back in his basket and gave a small contented huff that could have been a snore if he had been less proud. Mabel reached for the light cord, Lin lifted the rosemary to take home, and Tessa took one breath that tasted of glue, tea, and the sort of promise that requires patience.

The hatbox watched from the high shelf. The wrong handle had learned its lesson. The room had too. Tomorrow would be for frames and labels and the odd emergency with string. Tonight belonged to the quiet that follows a truth set in order, and to a small envelope in a safe, waiting for the next page.

Author's Note

Thanks for reading The Teacup with the Wrong Handle. If you solved the puzzle before Tessa did, I raise a cup in your direction.

This series lives on three pillars: fair clues in plain sight, a village that feels lived in, and tea hot enough to keep sense intact. Fernvale's hall, notice board, charity shop shelves, and a small repair bench gave me the tools. From there, Tessa, Mabel, Bramble, and DI Shaw behaved like themselves and refused shortcuts. Good. Cozy does not mean careless.

A quick word on the nerdy bits. The adhesives, wipes, and wood finishes are drawn from real conservation habits, then nudged into fiction. If you're tempted to test solvents on heirlooms, please don't. Ask a professional restorer, or, better yet, leave the patina alone.

Thank you to librarians and indie booksellers who press mysteries into the right hands, and to readers who love clue maps as much as characters. Gratitude as well to museum techs, framers, caretakers, gardeners, and all the patient people who keep old buildings upright and open for weddings, choir practices, and the odd village drama. Your quiet craft is story fuel.

Where we go next: the ledger stub and brass laurel tab are not ornaments. "Canal Gate, phase one" hints at a larger programme, tidy on paper and messy in practice. Tessa intends to mind her shop, label hooks, walk the dog, and keep her head down. Life in villages seldom allows that for long.

If you have thoughts, theories, or a favourite vintage teacup of your own, I love hearing from readers. Thank you for spending time in Fernvale. I'll keep the kettle on.

Liora Dawn

Printed in Dunstable, United Kingdom

76285263R00118